NANCY

VANDAL!

Suddenly, the elevator opened on our floor. Right away, I could tell something was wrong. I was the last one out when we left this morning, and I'd closed the door. Now it was hanging open by a few inches.

I put my finger to my lips and pointed to the door. George and Bess went silent, and we crept slowly forward. Bess took her cell phone out of her pocket and started dialing—hotel security, I was certain. George slipped off one shoe and held it above her head like a club. *One*, I mouthed to the girls . . . *two* . . . we all took a breath. *Three!*

I swung open the door and my mouth gaped open at the sight in front of me.

NANCY DREW

girl detective®

THE HARDY BOYS

UNDERCOVER BROTHERS®

Available from Aladdin Paperbacks

GIRL DETECTIVE ®

NANCY DREW
AND THE
UNDERCOVER BROTHERS ®
HARDY BOYS
Super Mystery #3

CLUB DREAD

CAROLYN KEENE
and
FRANKLIN W. DIXON

Aladdin Paperbacks
NEW YORK LONDON TORONTO SYDNEY

This book is a work of fiction. Any references to historical events, real people, or real locales are used fictitiously. Other names, characters, places, and incidents are the product of the authors' imagination, and any resemblance to actual events or locales or persons, living or dead, is entirely coincidental.

ALADDIN PAPERBACKS

An imprint of Simon & Schuster Children's Publishing Division

1230 Avenue of the Americas, New York, NY 10020

Copyright © 2009 by Simon & Schuster, Inc.

All rights reserved, including the right of reproduction in whole or in part in any form.

NANCY DREW, NANCY DREW: GIRL DETECTIVE, THE HARDY BOYS, THE HARDY BOYS MYSTERY STORIES, HARDY BOYS UNDERCOVER BROTHERS, ALADDIN PAPERBACKS, and related logo are registered trademarks of Simon & Schuster, Inc.

Designed by Karin Paprocki

The text of this book was set in Meriden.

Manufactured in the United States of America

First Aladdin Paperbacks edition May 2009

6 8 10 9 7

Library of Congress Control Number 2008941897

ISBN: 978-1-4169-7871-8

1012 OFF

CONTENTS

CLUB DREAD

SHOPPING FOR TROUBLE

"No!" George said. It looked like she was about to run. I stepped between her and the door, while Bess snuck up behind her. She wasn't going to get away that easily. We were doing this for her own good. She needed a new bathing suit, no matter what she said. Her old one was falling apart. When she realized we had her surrounded, George slumped her shoulders and let Bess march her back into the changing room, with a stack of swimwear in hand. I stood outside and waited.

George Fayne and Bess Martin were my two best friends. They're cousins, and in some ways, they are a lot alike. They're both smart and fearless and loyal and handy. George is great with computers, and Bess has never met a machine she can't take apart and put back together in five minutes flat. But when it comes to clothes, they couldn't be more different.

George is all about function, and would happily have worn jeans and a T-shirt every day of the week. Bess lives for fashion, and though her favorite thing to do is to cut up and resew an old outfit into something new, she wouldn't turn down an excuse to go shopping—like our upcoming all-expenses-paid trip to the Wetlands, the exclusive, environmentally friendly resort in the Florida Everglades. It was supposed to be one of the most exciting new eco-resorts, promoting "green" tourism.

My dad, Carson Drew, is a lawyer in River Heights, which is pretty far from Florida. But Jack Thorton, the owner of the Wetlands, is an old friend of his. Dad had done some legal work for Mr. Thorton, and in return, Mr. Thorton had offered us a free week's vacation. Dad had a big case coming up, so he couldn't make it, but he said I could go—so long as I promised to stay out of trouble, and to bring Bess and George to look after me. I've got a bit of a reputation for solving mysteries. Unfortunately, to solve them, I have to get caught in the middle, and I've had more than a few close calls. But this vacation was going to be all about sun, sand, and swimming.

Which was why we were at the River Heights Mall, trying on the latest swimsuits at Paradise Found, the new beach store that had just opened up for the season. I'd already picked out a one-piece bathing suit and matching hat in sky blue, my favorite color. Now Bess and I were attempting to wrangle George into trying some things on. We'd tricked her into the store by pointing out their display of high-performance waterproof sandals. Ever since she'd heard about the trip, George had been wild to explore the swamps around the resort.

"Did you know there are more than ten thousand tiny islands that make up the Everglades? And that tons of different plants and animals live there, from orchids to alligators to manatees?" George had spent the last week constantly reading us facts off Wikipedia. In fact, she'd even been using her phone's web browser to look things up while we were at the mall, which was why she didn't notice Bess picking out bathing suits for her until it was too late to get away.

Bess and George eventually emerged from the changing room. George's short brown hair was spiky and tousled, and with the brown-and-blue-microfiber deep-sea bathing suit she had on, it was easy to imagine her exploring the swamp or kayaking in the ocean. Bess, with her flowing blond hair and pink floral bikini, looked as though she had just stepped out of a swimsuit catalog. In fact, Bess almost always looks like she's just been modeling in a photo shoot. Sometimes it's hard being a mere mortal around her, but Bess was so sweet that it's impossible to be jealous of her.

"Look!" said George excitedly. "My suit has two hidden waterproof compartments to hold a map and compass." She pulled on the fabric of the suit to show the concealed pockets sewn into the lining.

So *that* was how Bess had sold her on the suit! I gave Bess a knowing wink as I inspected George's pockets. George loves any sort of techie gadget, or anything that allows her to carry gadgets and tools with her at all times.

"And the best part is that both suits are on sale. Two for the price of one," Bess chimed in. This was our last stop at the mall before heading back home, and we'd done pretty well. Bess and George changed back into their regular clothes, and we headed to the cashier, excited to be that much closer to our dream vacation.

"I can't believe we leave in two days," Bess said as we loaded our shopping bags into the trunk of my car. We'd stocked up on everything—suntan lotion, books, magazines, towels, sunglasses.

"I know," I said. "It's going to be great. I can't wait to relax on the beach."

Bess picked our sunglasses from the trunk and handed them out. We'd each gotten oversize round glasses with plastic frames. Mine were blue, Bess's were pink, and George's were a dark green. Bess assured us they were very *in* right now, even though I thought we looked a little silly.

"Hey, did you know the Everglades are really just one very slow-moving river?" George called out, looking at her phone.

"Can you look up the Wetlands Resort, George?" I asked as we all piled into the car. Dad had given me a brochure full of beautiful photos of the resort and the surrounding area, but I wanted to find out as much as I could about the hotel before we showed up. I liked to be prepared.

"Sure thing," George answered. I heard some rapid-fire tapping from the backseat. "Well, they opened about a year ago, and it seems everyone is raving about them. They're doing great things for both the Everglades and the local economy. They're the first big luxury resort to be carbon neutral."

"Carbon neutral?" Bess said. I noticed she was twirling a lock of her hair around her finger, a sign that she was thinking about anything. She gets nervous when I drive, and for no real reason. I haven't even come close to hitting something in days. Weeks, even. But you back up into one parking meter, and no one ever lets you forget it.

"That means they prevent as much carbon dioxide pollution as they cause. Apparently, they use all kinds of solar panels and easily recyclable materials," George answered.

"That's awesome," I said. Now I was even more excited to go.

Back at the house, Hannah Gruen and my dad were just sitting down to lunch. Hannah is our housekeeper, cook, and general miracle worker. I'm a lot like my dad—when we get caught up in a case, we both forget to do anything else, even eat. Hannah keeps us alive.

"Just in time," Hannah said as we came through the door with all our bags. "Sit down and have a bite to eat."

"Thanks, Hannah!" Bess and George said in unison. Hannah's a great cook, so Bess and George never miss a chance to eat at my house. We all took our places at the long dining room table. There was a big bowl in the middle, filled with dark green arugula, bright red cherry tomatoes, slices of carrot, and tons and tons of grilled chicken. My mouth watered just looking at it.

"How did the shopping go, girls?" Dad looked up from the newspaper he was reading. I knew he was sad that he wouldn't get to go down to the Wetlands, but he was still excited for us.

"Great," Bess said. "We even managed to get George into a new swimsuit!"

"It's made from a deep-sea microfiber!" George said. "And it has pockets!" Bess laughed and stuck her tongue out at George.

Dad smiled.

"Bess, George—you'll make sure Nancy eats properly while you're down there, right?" Hannah chimed in. "And that she puts on her sunscreen. Even when it's cloudy. I saw on the television last week that you can still get sunburned on a cloudy day. My cousin once got sunburned so badly, she couldn't sit down for a week. And that's the truth."

I laughed. Hannah's family seemed to be the most accident-prone people on the planet. She always has a story about some terrible injury someone got by doing just what you're about to do—and by ignoring her advice, of course. But what would I do without her to take care of me?

"Nancy, I want you let me know when you get down there safely," Dad said. "And make sure to let Jack know that I'm sorry I couldn't make it. Tell him to come up and visit us in River Heights sometime."

I promised that I would. We finished lunch, talking excitedly about our trip the entire time. Bess and George left to go home and finish packing. I hadn't even started yet. I needed to get on that, tonight. All I had ready was my purse, which always has in it everything I needed for doing a little detective work—flashlight, safety pins, evidence container, latex gloves. It pays to be prepared.

After lunch, Hannah went out food shopping. I washed the dishes in the kitchen while Dad dried them. I liked when we got to spend time together, just the two of us. It didn't happen often enough.

"Nancy?" Dad's voice was serious now.

"Yes?" I was pretty sure I knew what he was about to say.

"Promise me you'll be careful down there. No looking for trouble, no mysteries, no danger."

"Daaad."

"Promise me."

"Okay, okay. I won't go looking for trouble, I promise. And I'll call you as soon as we get down to the hotel."

Dad smiled at me and went back to doing the dishes. I was happy I could make him feel better. I knew he worried about me a lot. But this trip was pure vacation. I had no plans to go looking for trouble. I didn't need to.

Trouble always came looking for me.

CHAPTER 2

JOE

AMERICAN TEENS AGAINST CHORES

"I can't believe you forgot your keys," I said to Frank. "You're slipping up, old man." One of the great things about my brother is that he's so organized, it's easy to make fun of him when he actually forgot something. The bad thing is it almost never happens.

"Shut up," Frank whispered. "I don't see you whipping out your keys."

"Hey! You're supposed to be the responsible one." I poked him in the shoulder, which was probably a mistake considering that we were dangling at least twenty feet above the ground. Frank's hand slipped off the drainpipe he'd been holding, and he almost fell into Mom's rosebushes. At the last second, he managed to grab ahold of the window shutter. For a moment, it looked like he was safe.

Snap!

The top half of the shutter pulled off the side of the house, leaving Frank dangling out above the lawn. I laughed so hard, I nearly fell myself.

"A little help here, Joe?"

"In a minute."

I put one foot against the side of the house and pushed as far forward as I could, until I could reach my bedroom window with my outstretched hands. I slid it open and heaved myself past Frank and into the house. I stood up and looked down at my brother. Then I started to close the window.

"Joe!" said Frank.

"Just kidding. Here you go." I bent down, reached out my hand, and pulled Frank into the house. We both crouched down on the floor, listening for the telltale creaks that would mean we'd woken someone.

The clock on my bedside blinked 3:10 a.m. I groaned. Another night of not enough sleep. We'd been on a stakeout, getting evidence on a smuggling ring that had been operating out of the All-Night Donuts Diner in downtown Bayport. They'd had a complicated system of sugary signals: lemon custard doughnuts were filled with laundered money, Bavarian cream with stolen jewelry, crullers with secret documents. With the photos we'd gotten tonight, the smugglers would be in jail by tomorrow afternoon. Which wouldn't mean much when Mom was trying to get me to mow the lawn and all I wanted to do was go back to bed. Tomorrow was Mom's "summer cleaning" day, and there was no way to get out of it.

Mom had no idea that we were agents for ATAC, American Teens Against Crime, a top-secret government organization started by our dad, Fenton Hardy. ATAC recruited teenagers to go undercover and solve crimes when adults couldn't. I'm not going to lie, being in ATAC is awesome. Most of the time. But this was our third mission this month, and it was getting harder and harder to keep Mom from suspecting something.

I started to get up and felt something sharp in the side of my leg.

"Oops," I said.

"What do you mean, 'oops'?" Frank asked. I smiled weakly and pulled my keys out of my pocket.

"I guess I had them after all."

Frank stared at me in disbelief.

"Ugh," he said. "I'm going to bed. You're in charge of fixing the shutter tomorrow."

I started to protest that *he* was the one who broke it, but Frank had already left the room and I was talking to myself. It was definitely time to go to bed.

*   *   *

"You boys don't want doughnuts?" Aunt Trudy looked at us with surprise from across the breakfast table.

"A world of no," I said. I must have eaten a hundred in the last week. My stomach turned at the thought. I would never eat a doughnut again.

"Not even chocolate frosted, with sprinkles?" She waved one beneath my nose.

Well, maybe I could eat *one*.

"So!" Mom was using her perky voice, the one that meant she had work for us. "After breakfast, we'll need to mow the lawn, trim the hedges, vacuum the entire house, clean out all the closets, mop the kitchen and bathrooms, reorganize everything in the basement, and check the batteries on all the fire alarms."

Frank and I exchanged a tired look. It was going to be a long day. Mom always went overboard on her cleaning missions, but I guessed it was doable if we worked all day.

"Then, after lunch, I've got a few more chores for you."

I'd spoken too soon.

"Oh, and before I forget, you boys got some mail." Mom plopped a thick envelope down in front of Frank. Across the top it read AMERICAN TEENS FOR ANIMAL CONSERVATION.

ATAC!

Frank realized it at the same time I did, and tore the

envelope open. He pulled out a letter with WINNER! written across the top. He began reading out loud.

"Congratulations and thank you for entering the American Teens for Animal Conservation's annual Animal Adventure contest. As our grand prize winners, you have been awarded an all-expenses-paid weeklong vacation at the beautiful eco-resort, the Wetlands."

Frank held up two airline tickets and a brochure with a picture on the cover of the biggest pool I'd ever seen. Lounging around the pool was a number of cute girls in bathing suits. Did I mention that being in ATAC is awesome? I couldn't help grinning at the thought of our new mission.

"Wow!" Mom beamed at us. "How did you win that?"

"We entered a raffle," I said.

At the exact same time, Frank said, "We wrote an essay."

Mom looked at us in confusion. Frank said quickly, "We entered the raffle *by* writing an essay. About dolphins. And pandas."

Good save, Frank, I thought.

"That's great," said Dad. "So long as you guys make sure you call home every day and let us know how you're doing."

I was always amazed at how good Dad was at acting surprised. He knew all about our missions, but he never let on. I guess that's part of what made him such a good police officer back in the day. Now he spends most of his time recruiting and training new agents for ATAC. We were the first, but ATAC has grown over the years. Now there are agents we've never even met. And they're even thinking about going international.

Frank pulled a DVD out of the envelope and gave me a nod. I knew what that was. ATAC always put our mission briefings on DVDs and video games. I hoped that whatever it was, it involved a lot of time at the beach. And the pool.

"They've included a 'virtual tour' of the hotel. Is it okay if we watch it before we get started on the cleaning?" Frank asked.

If we'd had to wait until lunch to get the word on our mission, I think I might have exploded. Thankfully, Mom let us go.

"Be quick," she said, but Frank and I were already jumping up from the table. I snagged one more doughnut, and we scrambled up the steps to his room.

I slammed the door behind us, and Frank flipped the DVD into his video game player. The briefing would only play once, and then the DVD would turn back into a normal tour of the hotel. Our missions always erased themselves at the end, just to keep them from getting into the wrong hands. We sat down to watch.

The picture opened on a group of alligators resting

in the swamp. *Man, I'd hate to run into those things in a dark alley,* I thought. The camera trailed through the swamp, focusing in on a bird here or a flower there, getting closer and closer to a complex of buildings in the distance that must have been the Wetlands. The ATAC logo appeared briefly on the screen, and a voice over started.

"The Wetlands resort is the premier eco-destination in the country. Since it opened last year, celebrities, politicians, and environmental activists from around the world have stayed there, enjoying its complex of pools, spas, restaurants, and roof gardens, as well as its unparalleled beaches, scuba diving, and swamp tours. Environmentalists love it for being carbon neutral, the community loves it for supporting the local economy, and the guests love it for being so luxurious. But someone isn't happy."

Black-and-white footage from a security camera appeared on the screen. A guard lifted up a purse to show where the bottom had been slit open. It would take a practiced thief to get away with that trick! The voice over continued.

"About six months ago, a rash of robberies began at the hotel. They started small—wallets, watches, purses. The situation quickly grew to include break-ins and a raid of the hotel's own safe."

Another image flashed on the screen—an empty

wall safe. It didn't look like it had been blown open. Whoever did that knew how to pick a lock. We were dealing with an expert.

"Recently, things have grown worse."

A poster of a young girl with long pitch-black hair and dusky skin appeared on the screen. Her eyes were a warm liquid brown, and I swear she was looking right at me.

"Wow," I said.

Frank's jaw dropped. She was beautiful. She was singing onstage in a huge stadium, wearing a heavy gold necklace, bracelet, and earrings. Across the top of the poster was the name JASMINA in purple and silver.

"International pop sensation and winner of the reality TV show *America's New Big Thing*, Jasmina was recently assaulted and left in a coma during a robbery at the Wetlands. Her jewelry, a priceless collection given to her by the princess of Monaco in return for a private concert, was stolen and remains missing. We've been keeping a watch out for the jewelry in known smuggling rings and pawn shops, but to date nothing has shown up. We suspect the culprit still has it."

The DVD showed a close-up of the jewelry. I let out a low whistle. It had to be worth millions—thick gold chains with diamonds and rubies studded all over them. The voice over cut in again.

"If these robberies continue, the Wetlands will be

forced to close. Already there is speculation that the buildings will be purchased and converted into a sewage treatment plant, a move that will almost certainly destroy the surrounding environment. The tourism industry is watching closely to see if an ecologically friendly resort can survive. If the Wetlands fails, it could have a dire impact on the Florida Everglades and the future of the environmental movement as a whole."

Now a smiling brown-haired guy appeared on the screen. He was big and preppy looking, kind of like a Ken doll come to life. A muscley Ken doll. He looked vaguely familiar. He waved and smiled like a candidate for prom king.

"Matthias Dunstock, another ATAC agent, is already on scene at the Wetlands. He is the lead agent on this case. You will make contact with him and follow his direction. We suspect that this may be an inside job, so do not disclose your identities as ATAC agents to anyone at the hotel. Your first priority is to catch the person responsible for these robberies. Recovery of stolen property—especially Jasmina's jewelry—is also advisable."

Sometimes, I thought, *the voice-overs in these briefings sound so strange. Like out of the 1800s or something.*

A final shot of the pool from the brochure appeared. Girls everywhere.

"This DVD will reformat in five seconds."

Frank and I turned to each other. This was going to be our best mission yet—bikinis, beaches, celebrities. If we wrapped it up fast, we could spend the rest of our week down on the beach.

"Are you thinking what I'm thinking?" I asked Frank.

"Yeah." He grinned. "Imagine how much school we would have had to miss if this mission had happened during the school year!"

Sometimes my brother can be a total dork.

CHAPTER **3**

WELCOME TO CLOUD NINE

We stepped off the plane into an incredibly beautiful, perfect, sky blue Florida afternoon. Bess could barely contain herself.

"I was meant to live by the ocean, I just know it. I'm a beach girl at heart." She did a little twirl. George picked up a fallen leaf from one of the giant palm trees (*palm trees . . . indoors . . . at the airport . . .* I couldn't believe it) and began to fan her cousin. Then she gave up on that and began to chase Bess with the leaf instead, until a security guard gave us a look that made them stop.

It was hard not to be giddy with excitement, though. We were finally here, and the weather report predicted clear skies and warm temperatures for the entire week. Even the airport felt tropical, with giant windows and skylights that let the sun in from every angle. There were bright colors everywhere: bursts of flowers dangling from hanging pots, purple and turquoise tiles along the walls, displays of sunglasses and beach balls. Everyone seemed at least 23 percent happier here than in River Heights.

"So what's the plan, girls?" I asked, as we carried our luggage out to find the car Mr. Thorton had sent for us.

"I'm heading right to the beach," Bess answered.

"I read that they've got these hover boats you can take out into the swamp," said George. "I'm going to see if I can get a look at one of them. How about you, Nancy?"

"I'm going to take a kayak out to one of th—" I broke off midsentence. I could not believe my eyes. Bess and George looked at me in confusion for a second, and then they saw it too.

"Wow!"

Standing in front of us, holding a sign with our names on it, was a beautiful surfer boy with long black dreadlocks. He was barefoot, tan, and wearing a necklace made of seashells, and was grinning from ear to ear.

"G'day," he said. "I'm Thatcher. You wouldn't happen t'be the three VIP guests Mr. Thorton asked me to wait for, would you now?"

I could tell by his accent that Thatcher was from Australia—or maybe New Zealand. He cocked his head to the side, and his eyes twinkled in the sun. I could feel Bess melting—she has a thing for guys with accents.

"I guess we would be," she said.

"Ace!" Thatcher said. "Hop in while I get my shoes on."

Behind him was a cherry red convertible with the top down and an all-white interior. A classic beach-movie car, the kind Marilyn Monroe or Lana Turner would have been driven around in. Bess let out a gasp—she also had a thing for nice cars. We all leaped in.

We hadn't gone very far before I noticed something strange. The car didn't make any noise when we stopped at a light. No idling engine sounds, nothing. I wondered . . .

"Thatcher, is this a hybrid-electric car?"

"Yep. Mr. Thorton had a special fleet of them made for the Wetlands. The only hybrid convertibles in the country. How could you tell?"

"I drive a hybrid car at home. It's quiet, just like this one."

"You're very observant."

"Thanks." I smiled. Forget diamonds—good powers of observation are a girl detective's best friend.

Bess and Thatcher chatted about the beach the rest of the way to the hotel, and he offered to take her out surfing sometime. Guys are always offering to take Bess out. She has a way about her.

When we finally arrived at the Wetlands, it was ten times as beautiful as the photos in the brochure. The entire building was built out of recycled metals, and it glowed in the Florida sun. On one side it bordered the ocean and the beach, on the other side, the tip of the Everglades. The lobby had a fifty-foot ceiling, with a bamboo grove growing in the very middle of the room. Guests from all around the world lounged on sofas and chairs, dressed in bathing suits, saris, and skirts. Tropical birds flitted around the ceiling, and a butterfly nearly landed on George's head as we stood waiting to check in.

"Hi," I said to the large man behind the counter. He was so tall, I nearly had to crane my neck to look him in the eye. "I'm Nancy Drew. I think I have a reservation."

"Ah yes, Ms. Drew, of course! We've been waiting for you. And your friends. I was told there were three of you, but Mr. Thorton did not warn me about how beautiful you all were." He smiled, but it was one of those plastic smiles that adults give to small children. I thought he might have had a hint of an accent, but I couldn't be sure.

He shook each of our hands, called another person over to watch the front desk, and then motioned for us to follow him. We walked quickly to keep up with his long strides.

"I am Andrew Nikitin, manager of the Wetlands. Mr. Thorton apologizes for not being able to meet you today, but he is away on business. He will be back in a few days. Until then, he asked me to be your personal guide. Allow me to show you to your room and give you a quick tour of some of the more unique aspects of our hotel."

Andrew seemed like a nice enough guy, if a little pretentious. He said everything in such a solemn manner, it was hard to take him seriously. I had to stifle a little laugh when he held open the elevator door and gave a slight bow as each of us walked in.

The elevator was on the side of the building. It was encased entirely in glass, giving a great view of the resort and the surrounding area. You could see out across the water in both directions. The swamp looked dark and mysterious; the ocean sparkling and bright. I couldn't wait to explore both!

"As you can see," Andrew started in, "the Wetlands is built in a hexagonal design, meant to bring to mind the hive of the honeybee, the most collaborative and highly evolved of all insects. The central courtyard area has a swimming pool, a natural hot spring, a one-point-two-mile-long jogging trail, and the Courtyard Café, which serves breakfast all day. I recommend the pecan waffles with our organic Wetlands brand honey on top. The second floor, which we are passing now, has our hundred-and-fifty-machine gymnasium, which is free for all guests. The third floor . . ."

I tuned Andrew out, preferring just to stare out the window at the beautiful courtyard below. It was full of people laughing, swimming, and enjoying the sun. The Wetlands seemed like a magical place.

Finally, the elevator reached the top floor. We stepped out into a small room with four doors, not the long hotel hallway I was expecting.

"Mr. Thorton has placed the three of you in one of our unique penthouse suites. This particular suite is called Cloud Nine. I trust you will find it adequate to your needs." With a flourish, he produced a gold card, which he held up to a sensor on the door immediately to our right. We heard the lock click open. Then he handed each of us a similar card.

"If you need anything, please don't hesitate to call me." He stepped back into the elevator and we entered our suite.

Floor to ceiling, the room was painted to look like the sky. Watercolor clouds nestled against flocks of birds, and it was hard to tell where the walls ended and the windows began. In the center of the room hung a golden sphere with many metal bars coming off it, each tipped with a lightbulb. The sun! There were three doors leading out of the room. Each opened onto a separate bedroom and bathroom. Even the beds were made to look like giant fluffy clouds.

"Nancy, have I told you how much I love your dad?" said George in awe.

"Seriously!" Bess added.

Our bags were already there waiting for us, with a note from Thatcher telling Bess to join him down on the beach after we settled in. We made a plan to meet back up at the Courtyard Café for dinner, then changed into our bathing suits (and our matching sunglasses, of course) and headed out.

In the lobby, we split up. Bess went down toward the beach, while George and I headed off toward the swamp. A sign explained that the hover boats were restricted to an area where the ecosystem was not quite as fragile and could handle motorized vehicles, while the kayaks were for exploring the deeper, more secluded parts of the Everglades. Proper safety equipment, including a life jacket and an emergency walkie-talkie, was required at all times. If you wanted to use one of the hover boats, you had to take a lesson first. George and I said good-bye, then she went down to the hover boat area directly below the hotel, looking to find one of the boat instructors, and I left the hotel and headed out to the kayak dock.

It was a quick walk. Within ten minutes, I was deep in the wilderness. Inside the swamp the temperature was cooler, and I got goose bumps along my arms. It was quiet and dark. The dense underbrush blocked out the noise from the nearby resort, and the hanging Spanish moss made the area both spooky and beautiful. The songs of hidden birds filled the air.

The kayaks were tied up to pylons in the water, with paddles and life vests waiting inside. Some were built for two people and some were built for solo rides. I looked around for an instructor, but the area was empty. I climbed into a one-person kayak and tied the bright orange safety jacket over my swimsuit. With a quick push, I launched the kayak into the water.

I went slowly at first. I'd used a kayak before, but not in a while, and I needed to relearn the rolling motion of paddling from side to side. Soon it came back to me though, and before long I was moving swiftly through the water, heading deeper into the swampland.

I watched a white heron balancing on one leg, stabbing into the water with its beak, fishing for its dinner. I thought about what we'd seen of the Wetlands so far. Everything was so beautiful. All of the employees I'd met seemed open and friendly. I couldn't imagine a more wonderful place to spend a week's vacation. As soon as I got back to the hotel, I would call Dad and tell him all about it.

The path of the water split in two in front of me, going to either side of a large island. I hesitated for a moment, trying to decide which way to go. Off to the left, I heard the telltale sound of another kayak, the *splash-splash* of paddles hitting the water. I rowed faster to try and catch up with them.

As I got closer, I saw that there were, in fact, two kayaks ahead of me—one with two people and one solo. The two-person kayak was in front. Something about the people in it looked familiar, but I couldn't figure out what it was. They were two guys, teenagers (to judge from what I could see of them), one blond and one brunet. The other kayaker was a larger man with sandy brown hair and tanned skin.

The solo kayaker began to paddle quickly forward. The two guys in front were obviously distracted, talking to each other. The second kayaker was directly behind them now. He lifted his paddle out of the water and put it back over his shoulder, as if it were an extra-long baseball bat. He swiveled a little in his seat, and I realized he was about to hit one of the boys in the other kayak in the head! With a heavy fiberglass paddle, a blow like that would surely be deadly.

"Watch out!" I screamed.

CHAPTER 4

FRANK

A MYSTERIOUS STRANGER

A woman's scream ripped through the air behind us, and both Joe and I leaped into action. Years of ATAC training had conditioned us to react quickly in an emergency.

Joe spun around to the left. I spun around to the right. And the kayak spun around, sending us both into the thick black water of the swamp. As I descended deep into the muck, I heard a third splash somewhere behind us, which I guessed was Matthias. I made a mental note to recommend to Dad when I got back home that they give ATAC agents more aquatic training.

I wondered who the mysterious screamer was. Maybe it was some sort of tropical bird that just sounded like a terrified woman. But I was certain I had caught a glimpse of someone with long reddish hair in a kayak behind us, right before Joe and I flipped over. I hoped Matthias was all right, and Joe. Joe is a better swimmer than I am, but he can lose his head sometimes, and this was not a good time for that.

Quickly, I stopped thinking about the screamer and Matthias and Joe, and started thinking about the water. More specifically, how I was going to get out of it. I thought I was swimming upward, but I hadn't broken the surface yet. The water was so choked with algae that I couldn't tell for sure which way was up. I hadn't had a chance to take a deep breath before I went under, and already my lungs were starting to burn. I thought about turning and swimming in the other direction, but what if *that* was the wrong way? I had to keep going, and if I hit the bottom, then I would turn around. I just hoped I had enough air.

Finally, I hit the surface—and one of the kayaks. My head slammed into the fiberglass body so hard, I saw stars, and I slipped right back under the water. My hands felt heavy, and I couldn't move my arms and legs in a coordinated way to swim. I had just enough time to realize I was sinking, and in serious trouble, when I felt a hand grab mine. I put all my energy into holding on as the mysterious screamer pulled me out of the water and across the bow of her kayak. I coughed up algae and water. My mouth tasted the way old socks smelled.

When my lungs were clear, my rescuer helped me turn over onto my back. At first, she was just a blur of red hair and blue eyes. *I was right, I had seen a red-haired woman*, I thought. Then my eyes focused and I realized who it was.

"Nancy Drew?"

"Frank Hardy?"

"What are *you* doing here?" We said it at the same time. I couldn't help laughing, even though it hurt a little to do so.

Girls made me kind of nervous at times, but Nancy's mind seemed to work the same way mine did. We were always saying the same thing at the same time, or realizing something together. She was maybe the only girl I didn't become a total idiot in front of. She was staring at me in disbelief, waiting for me to say something.

"You—I mean, we . . . uh, that is . . ." I coughed up some more water. Maybe it was an exaggeration to say I didn't become a total idiot in front of Nancy. I became half an idiot. I tried to speak again. But what was I going to tell her? It was odd that we were even out in the swamp in the first place. Matthias had insisted we take the kayaks out. We'd been at the Wetlands for three days and we hadn't found a lead yet.

Then I realized I didn't see Matthias anywhere—or Joe!

"Joe! Where are Joe and Matthias?" I stared down

into the water, looking for signs of motion, but it was still.

"Matthias? Is he the guy who was trying to kill you?" Nancy asked.

"Trying to kill us? What are you talking about?" Joe said. He and Matthias had swum up behind us while we were talking, and now they hung off the side of the kayak. Joe seemed unsurprised to find Nancy here. He was always trying to act smooth around girls. And this wasn't the first time we'd started an investigation only to find Nancy Drew in the middle of it.

"He had his paddle raised like a baseball bat," Nancy said. "It looked like he was about to take a swing at your head, Joe. That's why I screamed."

"Oh," said Joe. "That's not possible. Matthias is—*ow*!"

Behind my back, I hit Joe's arm to cut him off.

"Matthias is a good friend of ours," I said.

Joe can be a little loose lipped at times. Nancy already knew we were in ATAC, but I didn't feel right giving away another agent's identity. And I didn't want the rest of ATAC to find out that we'd blown our cover.

"Yes," added Matthias. "Joe and Frank and I go way back. Who are *you*?"

Matthias was smiling, but he definitely seemed irritated. Probably because he was soaking wet.

Nancy gave him a hard look. Then she seemed to soften.

"Nancy—Nancy Drew. I'm friends with Joe and Frank too. I'm staying at the Wetlands for the week. I'm sorry I screamed. It just . . . it looked strange."

"I can imagine it did," said Matthias. "She's right. I did have my paddle raised in the air. I was trying to knock a water snake off it. They're rare, but some of the ones around here can be pretty poisonous. Which reminds me—we should get out of the water and head back to the resort."

We all got back into our kayaks and started paddling home. Joe, Matthias, and I were soaked to the skin. I could tell from the look on her face that Nancy wanted to ask us questions, but she held back—probably because Matthias was around.

"Are you here by yourself?" Joe asked Nancy. He was trying to be smooth again. He'd been crazy about Nancy's friend Bess since we all met at the Rockapazooma concert.

"No, George and Bess are here too. It's our all-girl vacation, since my dad couldn't come," Nancy said. "What about you guys?"

Joe didn't answer. I stuttered, not sure what to tell her. I didn't want to lie to her, but I couldn't tell her the truth. Not with Matthias around, anyway. I could give her the same cover story we gave Mom, about winning the essay contest, but if Nancy saw us working at the hotel, she'd know it was a lie.

For our cover, Joe and I were working as busboys in the various resort restaurants. The robberies were most likely an inside job. Matthias had already checked on the repeat guests—no guest had been at the hotel at the time of every single burglary. Matthias wanted us to keep our ears open among the staff and see if anyone said anything suspicious.

After a moment, Matthias spoke up. "They wanted to see the Everglades. Since I've worked here for a while, and we needed some extra help, I talked one of the managers into hiring them for a few weeks."

"Oh, that's cool," said Nancy. I could tell she didn't believe him for a second.

We got back to the dock and tied up our kayaks. Thanks to the heat, we'd pretty much dried out already, but I couldn't wait to get back to my room and take a shower. I could feel the swamp muck drying in my ears.

"I'm supposed to meet George and Bess for dinner, but do you guys want to meet tomorrow during the day?" Nancy said when we were done with the kayaks.

"Sure," Matthias answered, before Joe or I could say anything. I saw a flash of irritation on Nancy's face, but she covered quickly.

"Great. Let's meet at the Courtyard Café at noon." With that, she was off down the path toward the resort.

I started to head back to our room, but Matthias stood in my way. His arms were crossed over his chest, and he tapped his foot angrily.

"So is she another ATAC agent?" he asked.

"No," I said. "But she is—"

"A good friend," Joe said, cutting me off.

"Yeah. And also—oof!" This time, Joe elbowed me in the side.

"And also, Frank's got a total crush on her," said Joe. "See, he's blushing."

I *was* turning red, but it was because Joe had knocked the wind out of me. I coughed, and Joe continued talking. "Don't worry about her, though. She won't be in the way. You know girls—she'll probably be down at the beach for the rest of the time she's here."

Yeah right! I thought. Once Nancy catches wind of a mystery, she isn't one to back down. It's one of the things I like about her.

Matthias uncrossed his arms, seeming satisfied.

"Well," he said. "I look forward to meeting her friends tomorrow. But you two had better get back to your room—you're working the dinner service tonight."

Matthias took off at high speed.

"Wow," said Joe. "He's a bit of a freak, isn't he?"

"He's an ATAC agent, Joe. He's just a little highstrung."

"Yeah. That's an understatement."

Joe had a point. Matthias was a little weird. But ATAC had put him in charge. Although, so far, all he had us doing was working for the hotel. The most interesting thing we'd investigated so far was a clogged drain.

"Come on—we need to get changed into our uniforms."

Joe groaned. "Don't remind me. Couldn't they have made us lifeguards? Or something a little cooler? All we do all day is run back and forth with trays of food."

It was true—all day, every day, all we heard was, "Order up!" and, "Clean that." Yesterday, I'd spent four hours carrying boxes of dishes out of the hotel's basement and stacking them in the attic. Then Matthias told us the management had changed their minds, and had Joe move them back to the basement.

Joe was right. Our cover was the worst.

"We're only here for another four days," I said. "If we don't find out some information soon, we're going to have to come up with a new plan of attack."

"Yeah. Maybe Matthias can have us mow the lawn to see if there are any clues hiding in the grass."

I would have laughed, but it seemed possible that we'd be doing just that tomorrow.

CHAPTER **5**

STORMY WEATHER ON CLOUD NINE

"Frank and Joe Hardy are here?" Bess said, lying on the cloud-shaped sofa in the main room of our suite. "I think they must be stalking you, Nancy."

George laughed. I tossed a pillow at the two of them, but she just laughed harder. After our long afternoon exploring the area around the resort, we'd come back to the suite to shower and crash for the night. It had been a busy day, and we were pretty tired. We'd all changed into our complimentary Wetlands robes—made of recycled, environmentally friendly fabric, of course—and I was filling them in on what had happened while I was in the swamp.

"Very funny. They're obviously here on some case

for ATAC. I don't know what it is, but I think I know who their main suspect is."

This got Bess's and George's attention. They stopped laughing and leaned in closer.

"Who?" said George.

"This Matthias guy. When I came across Frank and Joe in the swamp, I was pretty sure he was about to hit them with his oar."

"What?" George stood up, her hands in fists. She's one of the most loyal people I've ever met, and she likes Frank and Joe a lot. I'd hate to be the person who messed with one of her friends.

"They're all right. But I definitely want to keep an eye on this guy. They said he was an 'old friend,' but they were careful not to mention ATAC in front of him. I told them we'd meet them for lunch tomorrow. Matthias weaseled his way into joining us, but I bet we can get them alone and get the real story. They're posing as hotel employees, so whatever is going on, it's got something to do with the hotel itself, not the guests."

"Well, Thatcher told me some things while we were at the beach," Bess said.

"Yeah?" said George. "Like his phone number?"

This time it was Bess's turn to blush and throw the pillow.

"No! From what Thatcher said, most of the employees

love working here, and a lot of them are immigrants that Mr. Thorton helped to set up and get them visas, like Thatcher. If this place closes down, they'll be out of a job—and maybe out of the country. I doubt many of them would do anything to hurt the hotel."

"Well, *I* found out that the hover boats are totally awesome," said George. "They run on giant fans, and they just barely skim the surface of the water. I took the safety course, so now I can take them out whenever. You know, if there's any sleuthing we need to do in the swamp or something."

"Well, we'll see what Frank and Joe have to say tomorrow," I said, yawning. It was getting late. "Between the five of us, I'm pretty sure we can handle any sort of mystery. But right now, I want to get to bed."

"Agreed," said George.

The next morning we all called our parents to let them know we'd made it safely. I felt a little bad not mentioning the case to my dad, but I figured nothing had happened yet, so I didn't have anything to tell him. Hannah told me again to make sure we all put on suntan lotion before we went outside. I was surprised she didn't try to pack sandwiches in my luggage.

It was cloudy, so we decided to stick around the hotel for the rest of the morning, instead of heading out to the beach. There was a lot of other stuff to do, anyway.

The Wetlands was like a cross between a hotel and an amusement park. There was a movie theater, a bowling alley, and an arcade in the basement, as well as a gym and a spa in other parts of the hotel. My favorite part of the whole place, though, was the garden.

The entire roof had been converted into an organic farm. They grew everything from flowers to oranges to sugarcane, almost all of which the resort used in their own restaurants. Guests could walk through the garden, or if they wanted, they could learn how to grow some of the food. The hotel even had it's own beehives from which it got honey. All the paths on the roof were solar paneled, to collect energy from the sun and turn it into electricity, which powered the hotel. At the end of our tour, we got to taste little bits of everything.

"This is amazing," I said, biting into a section of the sweetest, freshest orange I'd ever had in my life.

"Try some of this," said Bess, holding out a long slice of golden fruit. It was juicy and delicious.

"What *is* that? It's incredible."

"Mango," she replied.

It was the best food I'd ever had. And most of it was just simple fruits and vegetables, straight off the vine. I was in heaven. Even the gardens couldn't distract me completely from the case, though. I kept my eye out for unhappy employees or anything out of the ordinary, but it was just as Bess had said: Everyone seemed pretty happy.

I must have checked my cell phone every five minutes, waiting for noon to roll around. If there was a mystery here, I wanted to be involved. Finally, it was time to meet up with Frank and Joe. *And Matthias*, I thought unhappily.

Joe and Frank were waiting at a table when we got to the café, but we were in luck—there was no sign of Matthias.

"Hi, guys. Cute uniforms," Bess said as we sat down.

Frank and Joe were wearing the standard Wetlands outfit: a green polo shirt with brown shorts and a brown baseball cap. Frank blushed a deep red and mumbled something into his plate.

"Thanks," Joe said. "And I think Frank says thank you too. But he might have been talking to his lunch."

Bess laughed, and even Frank had to smile at the sound of it. No guy can resist Bess's laugh.

"You look awful," Frank said. "Nice! I meant, nice. You look *awfully nice*."

This time we all laughed, but I worried that Frank might not open his mouth again for the rest of lunch. However, once I asked him the real reason they were at the Wetlands, he seemed to forget his embarrassment.

"There's been a string of robberies in the last six months. Recently, they started turning violent. A few weeks ago, one of the guests, a singer named Jasmina, was robbed and left in a coma. Apparently, the Wetlands has been losing business ever since."

"I remember when that happened!" said Bess. "We were supposed to go to her concert in River Heights, but it was cancelled. It was all over the news. Her jewelry was rumored to be worth millions."

I remembered that case too. No wonder ATAC had been called in—she was a pretty big name.

"So Matthias is one of your suspects?" I asked.

"No," said Joe. "He's another ATAC agent."

I was shocked. Matthias, an agent? He seemed so untrustworthy. If he gave me four quarters for a dollar, I'd count the change. Twice. Maybe I'd misunderstood the situation in the swamp, but I still didn't get a good vibe from him.

"Where is he now? Investigating? Do you have any leads?" If we were going to work on this as a team, I wanted to know what was up.

"Actually, I don't know where he is," Frank said. "But we didn't tell him about you. Or that you knew about ATAC."

"Yeah, some of the other agents aren't as cool as we are about these things," Joe added.

"You mean you don't want anyone to know that we totally figured out about your secret club?" George couldn't resist rubbing their faces in it a little bit.

Frank and Joe had tried to hide ATAC from us at first, before they realized how useful we could be. I can understand why, though. If everyone knew about ATAC, they'd never be able to solve any crimes.

"We do want your help on this," Joe continued, ignoring George as best he could. "The only lead we've gotten so far is that Jasmina spent a lot of time at the hotel spa. Like, every day. Since our cover has us being busboys, we don't have a way of getting in there. Do you think you three could go check it out for us?"

"Could we ever!" said Bess.

The spa at the Wetlands was a five-star destination in and of itself. Guests came from around the world just to go to it. From the photos we'd seen in the brochure, it looked like a tiny palace hidden in the middle of a jungle—all inside the hotel. Bess had been dying to go to the spa ever since she'd first heard we were coming to the resort. I had to admit, I was a little curious too. And if we could pick up some clues while we were there, all the better.

"Great!" said Frank. "No one seems to have gotten to know Jasmina, and the official police investigation turned up nothing. It was the most recent—and the most violent—of the break-ins, so finding out what happened to her is our best shot at figuring out who's behind all of this."

"I might skip out on that, if you guys don't mind," said

George. "I want to take one of the hover boats out."

"Excellent!" A new voice came from behind my back. "Then I can take you out. You must be one of the lovely friends of Ms. Drew that Frank and Joe told me so much about."

When I turned around, Matthias was there smiling, his hand extended to shake George's. I wondered how much he had heard of our conversation. Even knowing he was an ATAC agent, I found it hard to like him.

"Matthias Dunstock," he added. "Swamp tour guide, friend of Frank and Joe Hardy, and very late for lunch. My sincerest apologies. So, what are you skipping so you can go out with me in a hover boat?"

Phew. So he hadn't heard much of our conversation. George looked at me and I nodded. She reached out to shake his hand.

"I'm George. I'd love a tour. I took the safety course yesterday, but I haven't taken one of the boats out yet."

Matthias smiled. He couldn't take his eyes off George. I still didn't like him, but if George went with him, maybe she could learn some more information about the case. Something had certainly put him in a much better mood today, so maybe we'd just gotten off on the wrong foot.

"Bess and I are heading to the spa," I told Matthias. "Frank and Joe, we'll see you later tonight?"

They nodded as we got up from the table.

"We have to get back to work anyway," Joe said.

As they started to get up, Matthias handed Frank and Joe a set of ID badges with their pictures on them. He explained that they were to wear them at all times, on and off duty. "Wetlands policy," he said.

George and Matthias made plans to meet up in an hour down by the hover boats. Only as we were leaving did Matthias acknowledge Bess and me. He seemed to have eyes only for George. The three of us headed back to our suite to get changed.

"I think Matthias has a crush on someone," Bess whispered loudly as we got into the elevator. Without looking, I could feel George's face turn red. She leaned back against the mirrored wall and tried to play it cool.

"He's just doing his job. And anyway, I figured if I went out with him, I could maybe get some information," George said. "And I didn't want to go to the spa. And—"

"Suuure," said Bess. "Sounds like a lot of excuses to me."

"We're just teasing you, George. You should go with Matthias. Just be careful." I didn't want to say anything, but I still had a strange feeling about him.

Suddenly, the elevator opened on our floor. Right away, I could tell something was wrong. I was the last one out when we left this morning, and I'd closed the door. Now it was hanging open by a few inches.

I put my finger to my lips and pointed to the door. George and Bess went silent, and we crept slowly forward. Bess took her cell phone out of her pocket and started dialing—hotel security, I was certain. George slipped off one shoe and held it above her head like a club. *One,* I mouthed to the girls . . . *two* . . . we all took a breath. *Three!*

I swung open the door and my mouth gaped open at the sight in front of me.

Our beautiful suite had been torn apart!

CHAPTER 6

JOE

DIRTY WORK

Doing dishes is my least favorite chore in the world, I thought as I carried another tub of plates and cups back to the kitchen. I dropped them into the giant soapy sink in front of Frank. We were on hour five of our busboy shift, and both of us were exhausted.

My apron was covered with food stains. Frank leaned against the wall and wiped the sweat from his forehead. He'd forgotten that he was wearing giant yellow suds-covered plastic gloves, and he left a white poof of soap across his face. I would have laughed if I weren't so tired. The kitchens were huge and noisy, with people coming and going everywhere. We hid behind one of the giant dish-drying machines for a moment to check in with each other.

"Anything?" Frank asked. He tried to get the soap off his face, but all he managed to do was smear it around his hair. He looked like a melting snowman. He shook his head, and the suds went flying.

"Nope. The couple at table three is really happy with their room, but they wish they had gotten one with a view of the ocean. The woman at table seventeen is reading *Moby-Dick*. And the family at table four forgot to pack bathing suits. But that's about it. How about you?"

"We're almost out of milk and carrots."

My job was to try and eavesdrop on the guests, to see if anything had been stolen recently or if anyone had seen anything strange. Frank was doing the same with the kitchen staff. So far we'd heard a lot of nothing.

"This is officially the worst cover ATAC has ever given us," I said. "Couldn't we have been guests?"

"I guess they needed us to be on the inside."

"Yeah, well . . . there had to have been something else we could have done. I *hate* doing dishes."

"I can't believe Nancy's room got broken into," Frank said, obviously trying to change the subject.

He was right. We needed to focus on what we were here for. The break-in at Nancy's room was the only lead we had.

Nancy text-messaged us right after they found their

room ransacked, but we were working and couldn't get away to investigate. No one had been hurt, and it didn't look like anything had been taken, but it had to be connected to our case. They'd moved Nancy, Bess, and George to another suite so hotel security could search the room. We needed to beat them to it . . . after we finished the never-ending pile of dishes.

"We have to get up to their suite and check it out," I said.

"It seems like a big coincidence that Nancy's room got trashed. I wonder if someone suspects that we're investigating this case."

"Investigating?" I scoffed. "All we've done is run plates back and forth for days. Someone would have to be psychic to know we're anything other than busboys. Maybe it's not a coincidence. What if there's a pattern we're missing? Maybe all the robberies occurred in certain rooms, or the guests who were robbed all checked in while the same person was at the desk or something. We need more information about the other guests who were robbed."

Frank was about to say something, but he stopped and pointed behind me. Katlyn, the kitchen supervisor, was heading our way. She would have been really cute, if she wasn't perpetually yelling and frowning. Her perfect skin, big brown eyes, and curly brown hair made her look like a cartoon princess. Then she opened her mouth, and you realized she was equal parts Cinderella and evil stepsister. I'd already tried some of my patented MoJoe on her, but she seemed immune.

"Hi, Katlyn. Have I mentioned how good that apron looks on you?" I smiled my brightest smile at her.

"Back to work—the two of you!" Katlyn roared as she ran past. I couldn't help noticing how beautiful her eyes looked when she was angry, but now didn't seem to be the time to mention it.

Frank shoved his arms back into the sink and started washing more dishes. I picked up my plastic tub and went back out to the dining area. Getting fired was probably the only thing that could make this situation worse.

Outside was a sea of happy, tanned faces. Was one of them going to be attacked next? The last person who was robbed was still in a coma. We needed to start figuring out this mystery, fast, before someone else got hurt.

Then I saw the manager of the Wetlands, Andrew Nikitin, sit down to eat and I knew exactly what to do. Matthias had introduced us to him on our first day. Nikitin had been going over spreadsheets on his computer, looking at records of all the hotel guests, for the last month. If the information we needed was anywhere, it was in his office. And right now, he wasn't there, which made it the perfect time to go get it.

I ran back into the kitchen, checked to make sure Katlyn wasn't looking, and dropped my tub of dishes and my apron at Frank's feet.

"Going to Nikitin's office—cover for me," I said. Frank was too shocked to say anything before I took off running. I felt bad leaving him like that, but he'd be able to come up with an excuse, and my chance to search Nikitin's office wouldn't last long. You have to strike when the iron is hot, or when the dishes are dirty, or however that saying goes.

Once out of the kitchen, I slowed down and pulled my ID badge out of my pocket. The trick to getting into most places is to look like you belonged there. If I tried to sneak into Nikitin's office, someone would definitely stop me. But if I just walked in—well, someone might stop me anyway. But I had to try.

Thankfully, no one paid any attention to me as I walked through the lobby, past the front desk, and into the offices at the back. Nikitin's door was closed, but the lights were on. I listened for a moment at the door. If anyone had walked into the hallway while my ear was pressed up against the glass, I'd have been busted in a second. Luckily, no one came and the office sounded empty. I tried the handle and the door popped right open.

I shut the door behind me and locked it—just in case. Nikitin's office was mostly empty: a desk with a computer on it, two chairs, and a few shelves of books and photos. The only light came from a lamp on his desk. There was no filing cabinet or loose papers anywhere.

As an eco-friendly resort, the Wetlands had tried to stop using paper entirely. It was a great move for the environment, but not so great for me—one of the best ways to get information was to look through the papers in office wastebaskets. Gross, but worth it.

I had maybe half an hour before Nikitin finished eating. I had to work fast.

The desk was completely empty of clutter. A computer, a lamp, a clock, and one stack of Post-it notes sat carefully arranged on the top. There wasn't even any dust. Inside, the drawers were neatly organized with supplies: staples, scissors, pens, pencils. It looked like a model desk in a showroom—not a single personal detail or anything out of place. I pulled the drawers all the way out and looked behind them, but there were no hidden compartments or envelopes taped to the bottom.

I was beginning to worry that I might have snuck in here for nothing. I turned to the computer. The screen was black but I could hear the hard drive humming. I moved the mouse and woke it up.

"Come on, give me something," I murmured.

A log-in screen popped up. His screen name was already entered—ANikitin. But the password field was blank.

I was in trouble. What would he choose as a password? I typed in "wetlands" and hit enter. A warning message popped up.

"'You have entered an incorrect password,'" I read. "'This computer will lock down after three more incorrect entries.'"

Uh-oh. I tried again. "Andrew." No luck. "Nikitin." The warning appeared again, letting me know I had one more chance. I had to think. I looked around the office, hoping for inspiration. There had to be a clue here somewhere.

Maybe he had a middle name I could try? Or maybe it was just "password"? Or "manager"?

I noticed a framed photo, the only one on the wall facing the desk. It was right where Nikitin's eyes would focus if he was sitting at the computer. I walked over to look more closely at it. It was a picture of a much younger Nikitin, grinning and waving to the camera in front of a beautiful gold-and-brick building with an onion dome on top. Across the bottom of the photo was written LENINGRAD, 1993.

I raced back to the desk and typed in "Leningrad." The computer whirred for a moment, and I crossed my fingers, hoping that wasn't the sound of it closing down for good. Then the desktop appeared.

"Yes!"

I clicked on the folder marked HOTEL RECORDS, and

it opened to reveal icons for spreadsheets and documents.

Jackpot!

But before I could open any of them, the doorknob rattled. Someone was coming in! I had just enough time to put the computer back to sleep before I heard a key in the lock. I dove beneath the desk.

The door closed. I tried to huddle as far back as I could under the desk, but if Nikitin sat down, there was no way he wouldn't see me. And since there was nothing else in the office, he was definitely heading my way. He must have been on his cell phone, because he paused by the door and started talking.

"Look, I'm telling you for the last time," Nikitin said. "I don't think this is a good idea. I think we need to lay low for a while."

Lay low? What was he up to? And who was he talking to? It sounded like Nikitin was involved in something shady. Now I just had to avoid getting discovered so I could find out exactly what.

Suspect Profile

Name: Andrew Nikitin

Occupation: Manager of the Wetlands

Suspicious behaviors: Wants to "lay low." Also, as manager of the Wetlands, would easily have access to every room in the hotel.

Danger factor: Seems pretty friendly. But if his job at the Wetlands ever fell through, he could be a strong man at the circus. Or possibly one of the elephants . . .

He started walking toward the desk, and I looked around desperately. There was no way out! I had maybe three seconds to come up with a plan. I felt something pressing into my back. A power strip glowed red behind me, and an idea hit.

I flipped the power switch and the room went dark. The computer fell silent. I held my breath and sat as still as I possibly could.

"Ugh. I think the power just went out in my office," Nikitin said. "I'll call you back in a minute, I have to go check the fuses."

Nikitin walked out. I took a shaky breath, counted slowly to five, and turned the power strip back on. I didn't want to leave any evidence behind. Then I ran out of the office as fast as I could. Our shift would be over by now, so I wasn't sure where Frank would be. Nancy and Bess were probably still investigating the spa, and George and Matthias might or might not be back from the swamp.

I went back out to the lobby, which was packed full of people, as usual. No one would notice me hanging out here. We needed to find out who Nikitin was talking to, and what he was involved in. But until we knew, we had to be careful—there might be more people involved. I typed out a quick text message to Frank, Matthias, and Nancy.

Think Andrew Nikitin is in on the robberies.
May have accomplice. Be careful.

CHAPTER 7

NANCY

MASSAGING THE EVIDENCE

Hotel security arrived at our suite before Bess, George, and I even had a chance to figure out if anything was missing. In fact, the place was so destroyed, it was almost impossible to tell if any of our belongings had been taken.

All of our luggage had been opened up and tossed around the room. The drawers had been pulled out of the dressers and emptied onto the floor. Someone had cut open the pillows and the mattresses, looking for who knows what. There were piles of stuffing and clothes strewn about the room. It looked as though a tornado had landed on Cloud Nine!

I wanted to search the room for clues, but it was impossible with the security guards there. We were allowed to take our cell phones, purses, and bathing suits, but they asked that we leave everything else untouched until they had a chance to investigate the scene. A few minutes later, Andrew Nikitin showed up.

"I am so terribly sorry for this," he said, looking ashamed. His head was bowed and his body stooped, making him look much shorter than he actually was. "Really, truly, you must accept my apologies on behalf of Mr. Thorton and the Wetlands. I don't know how such a thing could have happened. We will transfer you to another penthouse suite immediately. That is, if you will continue to stay with us. If not, we will of course pay for your lodging at any other hotel in the area."

Leave now? Just when things were starting to heat up? No way.

"Thank you, but of course we'll stay," I told him. "This wasn't your fault." Bess and George hurried to agree.

"We'll have a new suite ready for you this evening, then, and all your stuff will be moved in by tomorrow at the latest. I apologize for the delay, but we do want to have the police look over everything for evidence. Procedure, you understand. Until then, everything at the resort is on the house—please, try to relax and put this terrible incident behind you."

"Bess and I were thinking of going to the spa this afternoon," I said.

"Excellent," Andrew said, clapping his hands together. "I'll alert the staff that you're on your way."

"Thank you!" Bess gushed.

We gathered up our things and left the suite. In the elevator, I sent a quick text message to Frank and Joe to let them know what had happened. This could be just the lead they were looking for.

"Maybe I should go with you to the spa," George said. "If someone is on to us, we should stick together."

"True. But whoever did this wasn't looking to hurt us," I started, thinking out loud. "In fact, the room looks less like a break-in than like someone looking for something specific." I didn't know what it meant yet, but this seemed important.

"I really do want to try the hover boats." George sounded a little guilty, but wistful as well.

"Do it," said Bess. "We're only here once. Just be careful and keep your eyes open. And if anything happens, call Nancy."

"Yeah," I agreed. "You shouldn't miss out on having a vacation."

I considered saying something to her about Matthias. I still got a sour feeling from him. But George could handle herself, and it was probably just the strange circumstances under which I had met Matthias that made me mistrust him.

With everything settled, we split up. Bess and I got

out of the elevator on the second floor, where the gym and spa were located, while George continued down to the hover-boat dock in the hotel basement, where she had arranged to meet Matthias.

At the end of a long hallway, Bess and I found the entrance to the spa. A giant round doorway made of frosted glass sparkled in the light. The word "spa" was projected on it in colored lights, and the glass acted like a prism, sending a rainbow of words all around the hallway. It looked like the gateway to an ice palace.

"I have a good feeling about this," Bess said.

She opened the door and we found ourselves on a platform high up in the air. A spiral staircase led down to the ground. The spa was a giant open room, three stories tall. The entire ceiling was made of skylights. One wall was made to look like a mountainside, with a sparkling waterfall descending from it into a deep pool.

All around, women lay in robes and bathing suits on plush beach towels. A few were swimming or standing under the waterfall. Other platforms rose at seemingly random intervals throughout the room, and atop them I could see women getting various services done.

Another woman greeted us at the base of the spiral staircase. Her hair was silver and cropped close to her head, and her face was deeply lined but somehow ageless. "Welcome to the Wetlands Spa," she said. Her voice was cool and calm. "You must be Bess and Nancy.

I was told to expect you, and to let you know that all our services are the compliments of Jack Thorton. May I offer you some açaí juice and a robe?" She held out two glasses filled with deep red liquid. Bess and I reached out hesitantly to take them.

"Açaí is a tropical fruit, native to Brazil and South America," she continued, as two assistants walked over to us bearing white robes. "Its sweet flavor and beautiful color have made it a popular drink in the region. As it is a swamp plant, we are experimenting with growing it here at the Wetlands as a nutrient-rich alternative to soft drinks and sodas. Enjoy." With that, she drifted off to welcome another woman to the spa.

The juice was sweet and refreshing, and already I felt some tension drain out of me. I felt bad that Frank and Joe were cleaning dishes and clearing tables, but they *had* asked us to come here and investigate, after all. We finished our glasses and slipped behind two bamboo screens to change into the robes.

"I wish all of your cases needed to be investigated here," Bess said. She rubbed the soft white cloth between her fingers. "Egyptian cotton," she noted. Bess knew her fabrics. We removed our shoes and put them on the waiting racks.

I wasn't quite sure what one *did* at a spa, other than lounge around. And it seemed impossible to lounge and search for clues at the same time. I'd never even been

60

to a spa before. Bess, on the other hand, had been to her fair share and knew exactly what to do.

"I think I'll start with a manicure," she said, looking at her fingers.

"And a pedicure." She wiggled her toes.

"Then maybe a haircut and a massage. Or a facial? I hear the kelp and cucumber mask they do is to die for. And I've always wanted to try a deep-sea mud body wrap . . ."

One of the attendants overheard Bess and took her hand to lead her through the spa to the manicurist. Bess was still listing treatments she wanted to try as she went.

"Keep your ears open!" I whispered as she walked away. Bess winked. I knew I could depend on her to keep her wits about her, no matter how relaxed she felt.

I walked this way and that through the spa, unsure how best to look for information. The ground was soft and warm beneath my feet. There was almost no talking, except for a few quiet conversations in some of the seating areas. For the most part, the spa was a tranquil place. My cell phone vibrated in the pocket of my robe. I flipped it open to a text message from Joe:

Think Andrew Nikitin is in on the robberies.
May have accomplice. Be careful.

Andrew Nikitin! He had been in our room after the break-in. If he was involved . . . I wondered what Joe had discovered. And who Nikitin might be working with. Somewhere in the spa was the information I needed—I could feel it. I just didn't know where it was.

Noticing that I looked a little lost, one of the attendants came over to me. She was a young girl, maybe my age, with deep brown eyes, warm brown skin, and pitch-black hair to her waist.

"I'm Ciara," she said. "Is this your first time here?"

"Yes. Does it show that much?" I laughed nervously.

"It can be a little overwhelming at first. Believe me, when I first started working here, I walked around for two weeks with my mouth hanging open. Especially when some of the celebrity guests would come through."

An idea popped into my head.

"Actually, that's part of the reason I'm here," I said. I leaned in and dropped my voice, as though telling Ciara a secret. "I heard that Jasmina used to come here. I'm her biggest fan!"

"Oh yeah, she used to be in here all the time. She was the sweetest thing in person. Used to come here after all her big concerts."

"Was there anything in particular she liked?"

Ciara pointed up to one of the platforms that rose

from the spa floor. I could just make out an empty massage table at the top. "Ask for Petrovitch. Though I can't tell you what she liked about him."

That sounded odd. But it was a lead, and I had to follow it. Perhaps this Petrovitch might be able to shed some light on what happened to Jasmina.

I climbed the long spiral staircase up to the platform. A very tall man stood at the top with his back to me.

"Petrovitch?" I asked.

He turned to face me. "Yes?" I detected an accent in his voice, but I couldn't make out where it was from.

"Hi," I said. "I'm Nancy."

He stood there waiting, his arms crossed. I tried again.

"I heard you knew Jasmina. I'm a huge fan of hers."

He might as well have been made of stone.

"I, uh, wanted a massage." I'd never had a massage before, but I couldn't think of anything else to say. Petrovitch didn't seem like the type to engage in idle chitchat.

He pointed to the table, and I lay down. His large hands touched my back, and I felt him knead the muscles of my shoulders as if they were bread dough. It felt unexpectedly good, but I couldn't get into it. I tried to relax, but my mind was on the case.

"You are very tense!" he said. "It's good to have a real challenge, for once."

"Are most of the people here not very tense?"

"Ha! They wouldn't know tense if it bit them. All the guests here, with their money and their easy lives. They don't know from hard times." As he spoke, Petrovitch seemed to get angrier and angrier, and his hands became rougher and rougher. In fact, the massage was becoming downright painful!

"They don't even notice us, the people who work for them—who do everything! We might as well not exist." His accent became more obvious as he became more excited. He clenched his hands harder and harder on my sore muscles. Finally, I couldn't take it anymore.

"Ow!" I said. "Enough! Stop."

My words seemed to snap him out of his anger and he stepped away from the table.

"I let myself get carried away. I am sorry. Sometimes, it is hard for me to work here. Please, let me get you something to drink." He seemed embarrassed and stared at his feet while he spoke. Then he hurried down the spiral staircase before I could respond.

I lay there for a moment, my back aching. This massage had left me feeling worse than I had felt before he started. Petrovitch was the first unhappy employee I had met at the Wetlands. Was he angry enough to take out his feelings on the guests? Perhaps especially so on a rich celebrity?

I sat up and noticed that Petrovitch had left his

appointment book on the floor. I was alone on the platform. Glancing quickly down the spiral staircase to make sure he wasn't going to be back anytime soon, I picked it up.

Starting at the beginning, I found many entries with Jasmina's name, and some with her room number. Petrovitch must have also been seeing her outside the spa. I heard heavy footsteps climbing up the stairs. Petrovitch was returning. I turned the pages quickly, looking for any information that might be important. Finally, I found the last entry with Jasmina's name—on the night of June 23.

That was the night Jasmina was attacked!

CHAPTER 8

FRANK

MAKING A SPLASH

"Where's your brother?" Katlyn yelled in my face. Her breath stank of onions and garlic. Then again, so did everything else in the kitchen. They were two of the main ingredients on tonight's menu.

I didn't blame her for yelling—the kitchen was a pretty loud place, with everyone running back and forth, the industrial-size dish dryers, and all the cooking noises—but she didn't have to do it in my face.

Joe had been missing for nearly an hour, though, so I could see why she was upset. It probably hadn't helped that Joe had tried to hit on her earlier.

"Uh, well, he was here a minute ago. I think he's out getting more dishes?" I put my head down and kept scrubbing, hoping she would leave me alone.

She waited for a moment, then threw her hands up in the air.

"If he's not back here in ten minutes, he is out of a job!"

"But our shift is done in five minutes," I pointed out.

Katlyn looked at the clock, muttered something under her breath, and walked away. Looked like Joe would be keeping his job. I was sure he'd be overjoyed to hear it. I just hoped he'd found something so that this wasn't all for nothing.

I never wanted to wash another dish again for the rest of my life. For seven hours, every time I looked up, another pile of plates was being poured into the soap-filled sink in front of me. My hands became wrinkled and waterlogged, even inside my rubber gloves. And once Joe was gone, I had to cover for him too, running out to the dining room, carrying the plates back, and then washing them. It was like spending a day doing chores for Mom. Only worse, because there weren't even any doughnuts.

To make things worse, Matthias showed up to give us our work schedule for the rest of the week. We'd still barely talked about the case—all he seemed interested in was giving Joe and me more chores to do.

"Where's Joe?" Matthias asked. It seemed to be the only question anyone was interested in asking. "Is he off investigating on his own? I believe we discussed this, did we not? ATAC rules explicitly state that the superior agent must be notified at any time if—"

"He's not investigating. He felt sick and had to go back to the room." I felt bad lying to Matthias, but he was such a stickler for the rules. And if we did it his way, we'd never get anything done. Plus, I was beginning to dislike him. *Ugh,* I thought, *now Joe's got me thinking like him.*

Matthias seemed almost pleased to hear Joe was sick.

"Tomorrow," he said, "we'll have a check-in to see how the case is going. Until then, remember to report anything you see or hear to me."

"Will do." *Yeah, right,* I thought.

"Oh, and, Frank?"

"Yes?"

"You missed a spot on that dish right there. Remember, a good agent pays attention to detail and gets the job done right."

I wanted to take my sponge and wipe that smile right off his face. Instead, I scrubbed the dish as hard as I could and pretended it was Matthias's face.

When my shift finally ended, Joe still hadn't returned. I thought about calling him, but if his phone rang at the wrong moment, it would give him away. I couldn't risk that. With no way of contacting Joe and no idea where he was, I wasn't sure what to do. Joe can get himself into trouble at times. But two people sneaking around Nikitin's office were more likely to be noticed than one, so I couldn't go looking for him. Besides, Joe was just as good at getting out of trouble as he was at getting into it. Or, at least, nearly as good. Most of the time.

I decided not to think about it and to go check out Nancy's old room. If Joe didn't find anything in Nikitin's office, then the break-in would be our only lead. By tomorrow, the hotel would have cleaned up the suite—and any evidence the thief might have left behind. If we were going to learn anything, we had to get in there tonight.

I took the elevator up to the penthouse. When I got out, I saw that there was security tape across the door and a Wetlands' employee posted outside. He was big and burly, but he looked pretty young. I'd have to try to bluff my way past him.

"I'm sorry," he said. "This area is off-limits for the evening."

"I'm Frank. Mr. Nikitin sent me to replace you." I held out my hotel ID for him to inspect. The important thing was to act like I knew what I was doing.

"But I'm supposed to be on duty until midnight."

"Nah, they changed the schedule, so you're free."

"But—"

"I mean, if you want to stay, that's fine with me. I'll

head back down to the pool." I started to walk back into the elevator. It was a gamble.

"No, wait! I mean, if they told you to come replace me, then I guess I should go."

Awesome, he fell for it!

We switched places. I stood outside the door, trying my best to look bored, until the elevator doors closed behind him. Then I ducked under the security tape and into the suite. The place had been thoroughly trashed. Anything that could be thrown had been thrown. The dresser was knocked over, the drawers had been turned upside down, and there were clothes everywhere.

My phone vibrated—a message from Joe. I flipped it open and read his text.

> *Think Andrew Nikitin is in on the robberies.*
> *May have accomplice. Be careful.*

So it looked like Joe had found something after all. He was probably headed back to our room, so we could compare information later. Now I really needed to dig up some evidence. I couldn't let him have *all* the fun. I had to concentrate and try to find clues among all the chaos.

Nancy said they couldn't find anything missing, I thought. That was strange. They hadn't even taken George's laptop, which was in plain sight. Almost all the other cases had been straightforward burglaries. None of the other rooms had been ransacked either. They had all been clean, the work of professionals. Except for with Jasmina, there had been minimal violence.

In Nancy's suite, it seemed like the thief had been searching for something. And searching in a real hurry. No time to be subtle. But what could he have been looking for? The girls were staying in the penthouse, so perhaps someone thought they had money hidden somewhere. But in that case, why wouldn't they have taken George's laptop, or any of their other belongings?

Maybe he was searching for information. Other than Joe and me, only one person at the hotel even knew who Nancy was: Jack Thorton, the owner of the Wetlands. Could he have been involved?

Nancy did say that her father had done some legal work for Mr. Thorton. Perhaps he wasn't happy with the result. And it would make sense that he would be working with Nikitin, since Nikitin was the manager of the hotel.

If Jack Thorton and Andrew Nikitin are the ones behind the break-ins, that would explain why ATAC didn't want us to reveal our identities to anyone working at the hotel, I thought. But it didn't make much sense for Mr. Thorton to put his own hotel in danger. And we'd heard that he wasn't even around right now. I was going in circles.

I tried picking through some of the piles of junk in the room. Pillow, T-shirt, jeans, T-shirt, pajamas.

I dropped the clothes and turned to look somewhere else.

I went back to the door. The Wetlands had a complicated electronic lock system, where each door was reset after the guest left. The sensor pad showed no signs of being tampered with, and there were no marks on the door frame, so it didn't look like someone had forced it open.

If Nikitin was involved, it was possible the thief had a key. If so, I wasn't going to find anything, and I might as well give up. But if Joe was wrong, maybe the thief had gotten in some other way. It was worth checking, since I was up here already.

I looked around, searching for another entrance. Off to the side of the main room was a set of sliding glass doors that led to a large balcony. Since the penthouse was on the top floor, it would be easy for someone to drop down from the roof onto the balcony and get in that way.

Sure enough, the glass door had scratches around the lock. Someone had forced it open from the outside. Maybe they'd left behind evidence out on the balcony. I pushed the glass door open and stepped outside. I was so focused on looking for evidence that I didn't notice the small step right in the doorway. The tip of my foot caught the edge of the step, and I fell down on my hands and knees.

Bam!

The rough surface of the balcony scraped my palms open, and my cell phone went flying through the bars of the railing and off into the night. ATAC was going to be mad about that. Our phones have dozens of special additions, including GPS and a walkie-talkie mode, and I'm sure they cost a huge amount to replace.

Staying calm, I reached up with one hand and grabbed the iron railing that ran all the way around the balcony. I started to pull myself up, but it gave way beneath me!

I fell right back on all fours, my hands stinging with pain. The entire section of the railing separated from the balcony and fell off the side of the hotel. I heard a splash as it hit the water in the pool below me. Thankfully we were above the employee pool, which was already closed for the evening. Otherwise, that fence could have killed someone.

What is going on?

If I had been standing up and leaning against the railing, I would have gone right over with it. From where I had fallen, I could see that neat cuts had been made in each of the metal bars. I froze. The hairs on the back of my neck stood up.

This was a trap.

I got up and heard a strange cracking noise behind me. The ground shifted forward and I stumbled right toward the hole in the railing. I just barely managed to stop before I went over the edge.

I turned around and realized . . . the whole balcony was coming off the side of the building!

Cracks had appeared all along the floor, and in a few seconds the whole thing was going to end up in the pool below. From this height, hitting the water would be like hitting concrete.

Crrrrrack!

The balcony gave one last shattering sound and detached from the building entirely. I leaped off it just in time. I reached for the doorway—and missed. My hand caught one of the drapes inside, and I grabbed onto it for dear life. It tore off the wall, and I felt myself plunging toward the ground. This was it. I was about to be splattered.

But soon the fabric pulled taut and I stopped falling. The shock of it nearly knocked my hands off the curtain, but I managed to hold on. I was about five feet below the now balcony-less doorway, and I could see that the fabric of the curtain had gotten wrapped around the handle of the door.

A huge splash came from below, as though a whale had leaped into the pool. Carefully, I began to pull myself up the curtain, hand over hand. I heard a tearing sound at the top, and I slipped back down a few inches. The fabric wouldn't hold much longer—every time I moved, I could hear it tearing a little more.

I had no way of getting in touch with anyone without my cell phone. Joe would have no idea where I was. Nancy, Bess, and George had all been moved to another room. The real guard on duty for this suite wouldn't be here until midnight.

I heard the fabric rip again. There was no way I was going to last until then.

CHAPTER 9

JOE

HANGING OUT

After my close call with Nikitin, I was feeling pretty good. Finally, we had a lead on the robberies. *And* I got out of washing dishes. Bonus! Now all we had to do was figure out who was on the other end of that phone, and this case would be wrapped up with enough time for me to get a good tan before we headed back to Bayport.

No word from Frank or Nancy after my text, so I figured they were all still busy. It was late, and the Wetlands was getting quiet. When I left Nikitin's office, most of the crowd in the lobby had died down, either gone off to their rooms or to the hotel nightclub. I went to find Frank in the kitchen, but the doors were locked, and when I peeked through the window, all I saw were empty tables and a lone janitor vacuuming the carpets.

If Frank was still inside, well, it sucked to be him.

Next I headed back to our room. Frank wasn't really the party animal type, so it was a pretty safe bet he wasn't down in the nightclub or at the beach. He was probably asleep by now.

The Wetlands treated their employees pretty well, from what I saw. Since many of them were immigrants, they offered housing to anyone who worked full-time. There was a whole compound within the hotel, separated off from the guest areas. It had its own pool, gym, and places to relax where guests wouldn't constantly be asking staff to do things while they were off-duty. All in all, it was a pretty sweet deal. I mean, not as cool as being a teenage superspy, but not bad for what it was.

Our room was dark when I entered, and I figured Frank was asleep. I tried to get to my bed quietly, but I stubbed my toe on the hard wooden leg of the bedside table.

"Ow!" I said. "Sorry, Frank, didn't mean to wake you up."

There was silence from the other side of the room.

"Frank?"

I turned on the light. Frank's bed was still made. I wondered if he'd gone off to search Nancy's room. I decided I might as well stay up until he got back.

We needed to make a plan of attack on Nikitin. Maybe I could get back into his office and actually search his computer this time. Or maybe we would find something in Nancy's room that we could go on. And who knew what Nancy would find out at the spa. She might not be in ATAC, but she was pretty smart. Not to mention way cute.

I decided to hop in the employee pool to kill time, so I changed into my bathing suit. I still stank like kitchen grease and sweat, and it would be nice to feel clean again. *I could get used to this,* I thought. When we got back to Bayport, I was going to try and convince Mom that we should rip out her garden and put in a pool. I wouldn't even mind cleaning it . . . sometimes. It couldn't be worse than mowing the lawn.

The night was still hot and muggy. It never seemed to cool down around here. I was excited to have a chance to get in the water. Thanks to our stupid cover, this would be the first time I got to go swimming all vacation—if you didn't count the time Frank, Matthias, and I all fell into the swamp.

But when I got to the pool, there was no lifeguard on duty and no one swimming. The gate was locked. It looked like I wasn't going to get to go in after all. As I turned to head back to the room, I heard a tiny splash. *Maybe someone is in the pool after all,* I thought.

I looked back, but didn't see anything. Had I just imagined the noise?

Then something large and dark came hurtling out of the air and into the pool. It looked like a big piece of metal, like the door to an oven. What was going on? Was someone throwing things into the pool? I leaned my back against the gate and looked around, but there was no one else out there with me.

Suddenly, there was a huge splash and I was soaked with water from head to toe. I turned around just in time to see a piece of the hotel sinking to the bottom of the pool. It looked like an entire balcony!

I looked up to figure out where it had come from and saw someone dangling out one of the hotel windows, up at the top floor . . . right where Nancy's room had been.

Frank!

I was running before I even realized it, my feet pounding away as my mind was still taking it all in. Twenty stories up. If Frank fell, there was no way he would survive. I considered calling hotel security, but by the time I explained everything, it would be too late. I didn't doubt that Frank could hold on, but whatever he was holding on to might give at any moment.

In the lobby, I stabbed the elevator button repeatedly. It seemed to take forever to come. A puddle of water formed around me, and I realized that the few people who were still awake were staring at me. One of the night managers came over.

"I'm sorry, but we ask that people dry off before they go farther into the ho—"

I thrust my staff ID at him and cut him off.

"It's a plumbing emergency. Code 372-A."

He looked confused. It was always good to quote regulations at people. It generally took them at least a few minutes to figure out that you were making it all up. And by that point, I'd be gone. If the elevator would ever come.

Finally the doors opened and I raced inside, leaving the night manager standing there scratching his head. I hit the penthouse button and waited. Never had an elevator moved so slowly before.

Hang on, Frank, I thought. *Hang on.*

I burst out of the elevator as soon as the doors were open wide enough for me to fit through. The door to Nancy's suite was open, and I ran straight through the caution tape. I wasn't sure where in the suite the doorway to the balcony was.

"Frank?" I yelled.

"Out here!" came his reply. I heard the sound of fabric tearing.

"Stay still!"

I raced through the room to where I'd heard his voice. I could see the curtain out the window, straining under his weight. It was going to give at any moment. I threw myself on the floor, braced one arm against the wall, and stuck the other one out the door.

Frank wrapped his hand around my wrist, and I did the same. The curtain finally gave way entirely, and Frank's weight nearly pulled me out the door with him. I braced myself and hauled him up the side, slowly.

When he was finally all the way in, we both lay on the floor panting.

"So," I said. "You need to lose some weight."

"Very funny."

"You decided to just hang out for a little while, eh?"

"Stop."

"Wanted to get a little air?"

"I'm going to go back out there if you keep this up."

Frank got onto his hands and knees.

"I'm just kidding! Jeez . . ."

"No, look," Frank said. He was pointing at the outside wall beneath the door, where the balcony had been.

There were grooves in the plaster. Someone had spent a long time with a sharp object, tearing away at the supports until the balcony was ready to give.

"This wasn't an accident." Frank reached for his pocket, then stopped.

"I dropped my cell phone. You've got to let Nancy know that she and the girls are in danger."

So that had been the first splash I heard! I texted Nancy, but didn't hear anything back. I hoped she was asleep already. Things were getting crazy, and I'd hate to think . . .

Then something occurred to me.

"Frank?"

"Yeah?"

"I don't think whoever did this was going after Nancy. They trashed the room, and they had to know that Nancy and Bess and George would be moved to a new one. This was a trap for someone investigating the break-in. This was a trap for us. Someone knows we're here."

Just when we thought this case couldn't get any hotter!

CHAPTER **10**

NANCY

PLAN OF ATAC

I woke up in the morning to a text message from Joe, warning me about danger. I texted him back, letting him know I had some news of my own, and we made plans to meet up that afternoon at the café. I guess they wanted to sleep in for once—this was definitely more of a vacation for me than it was for them. Something must have gone down in the night, but I'd have to wait a few hours to find out what.

I looked around. Our new suite was even more beautiful than the first. This one had an underwater theme. One whole wall was a giant aquarium, with all kinds of fish, from tiny pink ones the size of my finger to a giant yellow-and-green-striped fish that was bigger than my head. There was even an octopus hiding at the bottom of the tank, trying its best to blend in with the coral around it. There were more than seventy fish in total. And I know, because I spent all morning counting them, too excited and nervous to do anything else.

"So you think this Petrovitch guy might be in league with Nikitin?" Bess asked me, leaning on one of the couches that looked like coral but was much softer and more comfortable. She was wearing what I thought of as her "action Bess" outfit—a pair of frayed jean shorts, sneakers, and a pink tank top. On anyone else, it would have looked boring. On Bess, it looked like it could have come straight from a runway in Paris. We were all dressed to investigate—shorts we could run in, our hair pulled back. For the time being, our vacation was officially over.

"Maybe. It seems like it would be possible. But we need something that would connect them. I mean, I've never even seen them together. But Petrovitch was pretty angry at the guests here, and Joe seemed certain Nikitin was involved."

George, as usual, was on her computer. I thought she was checking her e-mail, or playing solitaire, or surfing the Web, but I should have known better. She was doing what she did best.

"It's funny—I can't find any records for 'Andrew Nikitin' anywhere," said George, her fingers flying across the keys. "It's almost like he doesn't exist. No address, no phone number, nothing. Sorry, Nancy, I can't get you anything on him. But I did find this.

"It's a newspaper article about Jasmina's assault and robbery. The usual stuff, basically what we already know. But listen to this: 'There was no sign of forced entry, leading authorities to speculate that the victim knew her attacker.'" George stopped reading.

"Hmmm," I began. "So if it was Petrovitch—"

"If it was Petrovitch, it would make sense that there was no evidence of a break-in, since she was expecting him," George finished.

I nodded. It did seem to fit in with what we knew. And perhaps the robberies were getting more violent because Petrovitch himself was getting angrier and angrier. One thing was for sure, I needed to talk this all over with Joe and Frank.

"How was your date with Matthias, George?" Bess asked, trying to change the subject and distract us for a while.

"It wasn't a date. I mean, not really," George stammered. "But it was good. He's definitely a little odd. Uptight, but nice. He showed me all around the swamp. There are some beautiful islands hidden out there. You'd never find them if you didn't know exactly where to go. And he gave me this present—"

There was a knock at the door. We all jumped, and then laughed at ourselves. We were a little bit on edge.

When I opened the door, a bellhop in a Wetlands uniform was standing there holding a silver tray. It was Thatcher again! He winked at me, and then bowed deeply, enjoying his uniformed role. He lifted the silver lid off his platter and held the platter out to me. On it was a small envelope. I opened it up while Thatcher watched.

Inside, it read, *You are cordially invited to dine today with Mr. Jack Thorton. 4:00 p.m. in the White Heron Restaurant.*

"May I inform Mr. Thorton that you will be joining him?" Thatcher's rich Australian accent rang out.

I nodded, too overwhelmed by the silly formality of it to speak. Thatcher smiled, tipped his hat, and left. I was curious to finally meet Mr. Thorton in person. Perhaps he'd have some insight on the robberies.

As Thatcher got into the elevator, he called out over his shoulder, "Oh, and if your friends don't have other plans this afternoon, there's going to be a barbecue on the beach today. I could give them both surfing lessons."

"Sure," Bess and George yelled out. Thatcher gave me a thumbs-up as the elevator doors closed. Looks like we all had big plans for this evening!

Finally, lunchtime rolled around. We were headed out the door when Bess called my name.

"You forgot something, Nancy." In her left hand, Bess was holding my sandals. I looked down at my bare feet and blushed. It was a sure sign I was on a case when I was too distracted to remember to put on my shoes. I was thankful for my friends at moments like these.

At the Courtyard Café, Frank and Joe were wearing normal clothes, not their uniforms. Today was their day off, and they were free to try and find some answers. Quickly, they told us all about what had happened to them last night.

"Wow, I'm glad you weren't hurt," said Bess, reaching out to put her hand on Frank's shoulder. Frank blushed beet red and seemed to swallow his own tongue. He coughed and took a big drink of water.

"Luckily, I came along just in time to save him," said Joe, but Bess was too busy patting Frank on the back to notice Joe. Once Frank stopped choking, I told them everything I'd learned the night before at the spa.

"So I think Petrovitch is in on it—maybe he's even Nikitin's partner," I summed up.

George showed them the article she had found about Jasmina's attack. It felt like we had all the pieces of the puzzle in front of us, but for whatever reason, it still wasn't coming together.

"We need something to link Petrovitch and Nikitin," said Frank. "But until we figure it out, Nancy, you might need to lie low for a while."

George laughed and mumbled something under her breath that sounded like "fat chance." She knew me too well.

"Yeah," Joe added. "This is getting a dangerous. If you had been the one out on your balcony—"

"Exactly," I cut Joe off. "*Our* balcony. Whoever set that trap already knows we're involved. If we back off, that just means fewer people trying to solve this case. Besides, I think I know just the person we need to talk to—and I have plans with him tonight."

I told Frank and Joe about Mr. Thorton's invitation. They didn't much like it, but they didn't have a choice. As lowly busboys, there was no way *they* would ever get to talk to him. And if anyone knew more about the robberies or the employees at the Wetlands than Mr. Thorton, I would be amazed. I'd try to find out as much as I could about both Andrew Nikitin and Petrovitch.

"All right," Frank said. "But leave Petrovitch to us."

"Be careful," I told them. Petrovitch was bigger than both of the Hardys combined. He could have bench-pressed them!

"Don't worry." Joe grinned. "I can take care of Frank."

Well, I thought, *Frank and Joe can take care of themselves. Most of the time.*

Bess, George, and I decided to head out to the beach for the rest of the afternoon. There didn't seem to be anything more we could do around the hotel. I had the feeling that, by the end of the day, we'd have some answers, one way or another.

I was standing to go when Matthias came running up out of nowhere. His hair was messy and he looked upset. His face was red and he was breathing hard. His uniform was soaked with sweat.

"Where have you been?" he barked at Joe and Frank. Then he noticed George was sitting with us and tried to smile.

"I'm sorry to interrupt," he said. "I've just been looking for Joe and Frank all morning."

"We had the day off, so we decided to sleep late," Frank said.

"For once," Joe mumbled after.

"Well, even on your day off you're supposed to be wearing your ID badges. I think we went over that in your staff orientation, did we not?" Matthias was getting worked up. His words were very precise, like a teacher's when he is upset and trying not to let it show.

"Chill out," Joe said. "I've got mine in my pocket."

"You do?" said Matthias. "Let's see it."

Joe fumbled through his pockets and came up empty-handed. He said something about forgetting to take it out of his uniform. Matthias started railing on him again about how important it was that they carry their IDs at all times. For an "old friend," he didn't seem to like Joe and Frank very much.

"We were just leaving," I said to Matthias. "Would you like my chair?" It was weird having him towering over all of us, looking so angry. At least if he was sitting down, it wouldn't be quite so uncomfortable.

Frank and Joe seemed embarrassed, even though it wasn't their fault Matthias was behaving so rudely.

"Oh," he said, looking only at George. He seemed to suddenly remember we were here. He ran his hand through his hair, trying to smooth it back into place. "You're leaving? I hope you enjoyed the tour yesterday. I'd love to get to take you out again while you're here."

"Maybe," said George coolly. Frank and Joe were friends of hers, and as much as Matthias might be cute, she wouldn't tolerate anyone yelling at them.

"I was thinking maybe this evening, if you don't have any plans, we could go to the beach, or out for dinner?"

"Actually, Bess and I have plans tonight," George said, linking her arm through Bess's. "But thanks for the offer."

With that, we left.

CHAPTER **11**

FRANK

MARCO POLOVITCH

Once Nancy, Bess, and George left, Matthias really got down to business. The business of chewing us out, that is.

"Where were you last night, Joe? I find it incredibly irresponsible that you would leave your assigned post in the middle of an investigation."

Matthias made it sound like Joe had left a stake-out, or something else important, not just a sink full of dishes.

"I had something bad, man. I was puking everywhere. You wouldn't have wanted me to stay in that kitchen." Joe tried his best to look sick, but it was pretty clear Matthias wasn't buying it. "It must have been one of those twenty-four-hour bugs. Maybe food poisoning or something." He coughed a little, for good measure.

I tossed him an eye roll.

"I am beginning to doubt how serious you two are about solving this crime. I've got to say, I was expecting more from the two of you. Everyone says you're the golden boys of ATAC."

"What?" Joe said. "That's crazy. We're just agents like anyone else." Joe realized he was starting to get loud, and pulled his chair in closer. It wouldn't be good for the entire restaurant to hear that we were secret agents.

Sure, our dad had started ATAC, but we never received any special treatment because of it. If I didn't know better, I would have said Matthias sounded . . . *jealous*. He must have been really nervous about this case. I guess it meant a lot more to him, since he'd been working down here for so long.

Maybe we were wrong to keep what we had learned from him—he might have been annoying, but he was still a fellow ATAC agent, and we needed to do our best to work with him. I decided to tell him what had actually happened last night.

"Look, Matthias, the truth is—"

"I'm really growing tired of your excuses," Matthias said. "From now on, I'd appreciate it if you two would follow my orders. Perhaps we could really get somewhere then. Now go get your staff IDs."

Ohhhh-kay. Maybe I didn't need to tell him anything after all.

Joe was practically shaking with anger, and I put my hand on his shoulder to calm him down. The last thing we needed was for him and Matthias to get into a screaming match in the middle of the hotel. We started to walk away, when Matthias called out over his shoulder.

"Oh, and, Joe? Try not to get any more *food poisoning*, okay?"

All the way back to our room, Joe kept muttering under his breath about Matthias. When we finally got there, he swung the door open and it banged against the wall.

"Hey, calm down," I said.

Joe looked embarrassed.

"Sorry. He just gets on my nerves, you know?"

"Yeah. But we've only got a few more days to get to the bottom of this. So what's our plan?"

I grabbed our staff IDs while we were talking. The photo of me was terrible—my hair was a mess and my skin was breaking out when they took it. The IDs themselves were weirdly clunky. Much heavier than I would have expected. I tossed Joe's ID to him.

"Let's find Petrovitch," Joe said. "Maybe if we talk to him, he'll let something slip."

"Yeah, like 'Oh, hi, I'm Petrovitch. I've been robbing this hotel blind. What's your name?'"

"Okay, hotshot. You got a better plan?"

He had me there. From what Nancy said, Petrovitch wasn't the kind of guy we'd want to catch us breaking into his place. We left our room and headed toward the spa. I figured we'd have to set up a stakeout and follow him to someplace where we could talk. But we were in luck.

"Hey, Frank, check it out—over by the employee pool."

The pool had been closed in the morning while the cleanup crew dragged the balcony out of it, but it seemed like it was open now. I turned and looked as we walked past. Huge, bald, and lying out on one of the deck chairs—that had to be Petrovitch.

Suspect Profile

Name: Petrovitch

Occupation: Massage therapist

Suspicious behaviors: Last person to see Jasmina the night she was attacked. Has anger-management problems. Hates rich guests.

Danger factor: Anger could easily get out of hand.

"So—guess it's time for us to go swimming, eh?" I said. Finally, this mission was starting to look up.

Joe tore off his T-shirt and whooped.

"Race you?" Joe said.

We ran to the pool. Thankfully, we were at the deep

end, so when we made it to the edge, I dove straight in. I could feel Joe doing the same next to me. The cold water came as a shock after the days of hot sun and even hotter dishwater. I surfaced halfway down the pool.

"Ha! Beat you, old man," Joe said.

"No way. I was *definitely* in the water before you."

"You wish!"

We drifted over to the side of the pool where Petrovitch was lying, debating as we went. We played water games for a while. Eventually, we got out and flopped down on two of the chairs, conveniently placing Petrovitch between us. Up close, he was even bigger than Nancy had said—like three people pasted together.

"Hey there," I said.

Petrovitch grunted and opened one giant eye.

"Did you see us jump in? Which one of us hit the water first?"

"Don't know." He grunted and closed his eyes. I could hear the accent Nancy had mentioned, and I felt a slight thrill—this had to be the right guy.

"So, do you work here too?" Joe tried to get him talking.

"Yep."

This time, he didn't even bother opening one of his eyes.

"We just started," I said. "Got any tips for new people?"

Silence. I thought he might have fallen asleep. So far, our fact-finding mission was a total bust. He had seemed eager to talk to Nancy. Maybe it was because she was a pretty girl—a totally unfair advantage. Or maybe we were just trying the wrong tack.

"Bleh. I can't believe we have to work in the kitchen again tomorrow, Joe. This job is the worst." Hopefully Joe would catch on.

"I know," Joe said, anger creeping into his voice. "And the guests—man! They act like we're not even people sometimes."

"Ha!" A deep rumble came from Petrovitch. I thought it might be a laugh. "That's because we are not people, not to them."

"Totally," I agreed. Actually, I'd found most of the guests to be really nice, but there were a few spoiled types who were clearly used to having people wait on them hand and foot.

"It just gets me so angry," Joe continued. "It's like, without us, there wouldn't be a resort. So the least they could do is be respectful."

"All day, every day, it's, 'Do this!' or, 'Get that!'" Both of Petrovitch's eyes were open now, and he had raised himself up on his elbows. "I didn't even have to work this hard on my family's farm!" He made a noise of disgust.

"Yeah, it's ridiculous!" I said.

Petrovitch was really on a roll now.

"No one respects the laborers. The people who put bread on their table."

"Right," said Joe. "I guess they're getting what they deserve now, with these robberies and all."

Petrovitch stopped dead. I could feel him freeze up. Did we go too far too soon? Did he think we were onto him?

"My friend, these are dangerous waters you are wading in," he said. "I have seen what happens when people think they can take these things into their own hands, and it goes to a bloody place. What we need is a union, not a bunch of thugs."

"Well, what about what happened to that singer? Jasmina? Wasn't she just getting what she deserved?" This was our chance, and I jumped on it.

"What do you know about that?" Petrovitch roared. "She was a nice girl! Whoever did that to her is an animal." He seemed genuinely upset about Jasmina. If he was acting, he deserved an Oscar.

"Someone told us you were close to her. That you had seen her on the night she was attacked." I tried to be as calm as I could. Petrovitch was beginning to draw attention, and I needed to keep him talking.

"Bah! I already went over this with the police." He

shook his head in disgust. "These filthy rumors. Yes, I saw her that night. But when I left, she was fine. And she had another visitor after me, a tall guy."

"Who? What did he look like?" I was too excited to hold my questions in. If someone else had been in Jasmina's suite that night, we needed to find him.

The loud ring of a cell phone broke through our conversation. Petrovitch pulled it out of his pocket.

"Da? Okay. I'll be there immediately."

He stood up.

"See? Even on our days off, they make us work. But believe me, friends, violence is not the answer to this. I'm organizing a union meeting next week, for all of us workers to come together. I hope to see you there."

"Wait!" I called after him, but Petrovitch was already running toward the main part of the hotel, taking the information we needed with him. We had been so close!

"What do you think?" Joe said.

"Nancy was right—he certainly is angry. But I don't think he was lying to us."

"Yeah, me either."

"We need to find out who was the last person to see Jasmina."

"Agreed." Joe looked longingly at the pool. "Maybe there's a clue in there?"

"Well, ATAC always tells us to investigate every

possible angle, right? And we've got some time to kill before we check in with Nancy, so . . ."

I leaped in. This time, I definitely hit the water first.

J O E

Please. I totally beat you.

CHAPTER **12**

THE OTHER BROTHERS

George, Bess, and I headed back up to our suite to get ready for our evening out. Matthias really knew how to ruin a party. I didn't understand how Frank and Joe could be friends with him, let alone work with him in ATAC. Poor George! He wouldn't leave her alone. Thankfully George knew how to let a guy know she wasn't interested.

"All right, Nancy, let's see what you've got." Bess dragged my suitcase out. She put it on the table in the main room and started rummaging through it.

"I don't think I brought any of my investigation stuff. I know I left the picklocks at home. But maybe . . ."

Bess was right. We needed to get ready. It seemed like things were coming to a head. Who knew what we might need.

"No, Nancy. Clothes! Let's see what clothes you've got. You're meeting with Jack Thorton later. You need to get dressed up."

I groaned.

"This won't do?" I pointed to my shorts and sandals.

Bess didn't even bother responding. She was right. I sighed and helped her lay out all my clothes on the table.

"Now it's your turn to let her play dress-up on you. This is payback for the mall." George laughed.

Bess threw most of my clothes aside with a shake of her head. We had different standards when it came to fashion. The pile of "no's" far outweighed the pile of "maybe's." Finally, she settled on a black shirt, the one pair of long slacks I had brought with me, and a pair of heels, which I almost hadn't brought but which Bess convinced me I needed. They were low, only about an inch, but I still felt like I was walking on stilts whenever I put them on.

"Do you think that shirt is fancy enough?" I didn't know a lot about fashion, but it definitely looked like a plain T-shirt to me.

"Of course not. I'm going to have to work on it. Hand me my sewing kit?"

I should have known. If *I* thought it wasn't fancy enough, I'm surprised Bess even thought it could be saved. But she was a miracle worker when it came to clothes. As I watched, she cut all along the bottom of the shirt, then took the extra fabric and began to stitch a fancy new collar.

George called home to check in, and I could hear her telling her parents all about the hotel and the beach, though she didn't mention anything about our room being trashed or the robberies. George was one of those people who could never sit still, and she paced back and forth through the suite while she was on the phone.

As she walked, I noticed a strange noise, like a buzzing sound. At first I thought it was her phone, but then I noticed that it only happened when she was walking near one of the sofas—the one that was shaped like a giant clamshell. Once George was off the phone, the noise stopped entirely.

I had a suspicion. I took a piece of paper and pen from my bag. Quickly, I wrote out two notes that said, *pretend to have a conversation*. I handed one to George and the other to Bess. Their eyes widened, but they nodded.

"Hey, George," said Bess. "So do you want to go to that party on the beach that Thatcher mentioned?"

"I think so. Do you think it'll be fun?"

"I hope so."

While they talked, I took Bess's scissors out of her sewing kit and walked over to the couch. I took out my cell phone and turned the volume all the way down. Then I dialed my voice mail. The buzzing returned. I began to pass the phone over the couch cushions, listening. The sound was loudest over by one of the seams. If I was wrong about this, I was going to have to apologize to Mr. Thorton tonight.

I slipped the shears in between the thread and the fabric, cutting each stitch individually to make the least amount of noise and mess possible. George and Bess crept closer, continuing their fake conversation loudly. I peeled back the fabric. A small metal circle was sitting there, glinting. As I watched, a red light blinked on and off. There were small holes at one end of it, like the kind you see on a pair of headphones.

The room was bugged!

We all looked at one another, wide-eyed.

We hadn't said much of anything today, but if the device was here yesterday, the person listening would know all about Joe, Frank, and Petrovitch. I pulled the fabric back up and stitched it closed again. Whoever had put the device there, we didn't want them to know we had found it.

We continued to make fake conversation until the time came to leave. Bess finished making my new shirt, and we all got dressed to go out. In the elevator, we finally stopped pretending.

"George, can you look up some information on listening devices and see if there is any way to block them out?"

"Sure thing, Nancy."

"Bess, I need you to let Frank and Joe know about this. And then I want the two of you to be careful at that party tonight! Someone at the hotel is after us, and who knows what they may have overheard."

The elevator doors opened onto the lobby, and we split up. I trusted Bess and George to look after each other, but I was starting to worry. Most of the cases we worked on were back in River Heights, where we could call on Police Chief McGuiness or my father to help us out. Here, I had no idea who we could trust. Other than the Hardy boys, that is.

A uniformed waiter with white hair met me at the door to the Wetlands main restaurant, the White Heron.

"Ms. Drew?"

"Yes," I answered.

"I have been instructed to take you to Mr. Thorton's private dining room. Please come this way."

With that, he walked off away from the restaurant. I hurried to catch up with him. We walked through the lobby until we arrived at a small door I had not noticed before. It was very plain, except that it had a large keyhole in it. All the other doors in the hotel worked on keypads and sensor systems. The waiter pulled out a large black key, and the door clicked audibly as he turned it in the lock. He beckoned me to enter, and closed the door behind me.

I found myself on a narrow path above a large pool. The water was lit from below, and I could see all manner of things swimming below me: fish, turtles, lizards, frogs. At the end of the path, a man sat at a table lit by candles. He smiled as I walked toward him.

"Nancy!"

"Mr. Thorton." I smiled.

"You must call me Jack. May I call you Nancy? Sit, sit!" Jack Thorton was a large, smiling man with incredible energy. He must have been as old as my father, or maybe even older. His hair was all white, and his dark skin was lined with deep grooves from a lifetime of smiling. He seemed so excited about everything that his words tumbled out of him in the wrong order, and much too fast. I liked him instantly.

"Of course, Mr. Thor—I mean, Jack. Please call me Nancy," I said as I sat down. The table was set with old, heavy silver and thin, bone-white china. The table was an antique as well, a grooved and scarred piece of hardwood that must have weighed a ton! Jack caught me looking at everything and smiled.

"This was all my mother's. Handed down through the generations, though my mother was never clear on how many generations there were. French aristocracy, she assured me, we were. Or sometimes Creole royalty. Or Seminole chiefs. Her stories changed, but the china stayed the same. When she died, it became mine. As did the land the hotel now sits on—turns out she might have been telling the truth all along."

Jack picked up a bell that was sitting by the table and rang it once. A waiter came in with two small plates. I smelled spices and onions. On each plate was a tiny crepe topped with brownish yellow eggs.

"Curried eggs," Jack said. "I hope you don't mind, I took the liberty of ordering us a tasting menu, a selection of our chef's favorites dishes."

I put a bite in my mouth. It was delicious!

"This is amazing. Thank you!"

Jack smiled and clapped his hands. For the next half hour, the waiter brought a steady stream of tiny dishes—a bite of this, a taste of that. Most of it I barely recognized, but all of it was great. I tried to ask Jack about the hotel, but the food was so good, my mouth was always full.

Finally, we took a break before dessert and I had my opening.

"How have you been enjoying your stay, Nancy?"

"It's been wonderful, Mr. Thor—I mean, Jack." It was hard to get used to calling someone my dad's age by their first name. I could do it out loud, but in my head, I still thought of him as Mr. Thorton. "You must hear this all the time, but I've never been anywhere quite this amazing before!"

"It's so good of you to say that, dear. It has not been

the easiest year for the resort, I'm afraid." His eyebrows scrunched up in his face and he looked like a sad cartoon character. His emotions were so big, they didn't look real sometimes. But you could tell they were genuine.

"Has something been wrong?"

"And here I thought everyone had heard! But then, we're always the center of our own universe, right? It's good to be reminded that life goes on aside from our woes." He sighed and wrung his hands. "There have been a number of terrible events here in the past few months: robberies and break-ins and balconies falling into the pool and altogether too much for me to be worrying such a lovely young girl about over dinner. Tell me, how has your father been?"

Just when we were getting close to the information I wanted to discuss, our conversation headed off in another direction. I told him how sad Dad was that he couldn't make it down to visit.

"Ah, Carson! That was always your father's way. Busy, busy, busy. Too big a heart to turn anyone down. That's how I knew he was the right person to help me out with my employee problems."

Employee problems? The only unhappy employee I'd met was Petrovitch. This sounded exactly like the sort of information we needed.

"What kind of problems were you having? It's hard

to imagine someone who works at the Wetlands not being happy. I wish I could work here!"

"Oh, no—no, no, no, nothing like that. I pride myself on treating my employees well. I know what it's like to work in the resorts down here. Some of them treat their employees terribly, like servants."

Mr. Thorton went on to explain that many of the people who worked at the resort were immigrants. There was a large immigrant population in the local community. It was normal for restaurants and hotels to hire illegal immigrants, who they could pay less and treat poorly. Mr. Thorton, with help from my dad, was working on a program to enable his employees to apply for visas, which would let them stay legally.

"Wow," I told Mr. Thorton. "That's really generous of you."

"It was all due to an employee of mine. I believe you met him, Andrew Nikitin?"

My skin prickled at the sound of his name.

"Yes, he checked us in. The program was his idea?"

"Yes, indeed. Now his is a sad, sad story." Mr. Thorton paused, and I could tell he wanted me to ask him for more information, which I was happy to do.

"Oh, really?"

"Yes, his life has been very hard. He himself is an immigrant from Russia. He changed his name to fit in better, from Androvitch to Andrew. He moved here many years ago, but still he sends almost all his money back home to support his family. His brother came here a few months ago, and we hired him to work at the Wetlands. But Andrew is still perpetually in debt."

Nikitin has a brother? My mind froze. I knew, for certain, who it was.

"I think I've met his brother—his name isn't Petrovitch, is it?"

"Yes, that's him!"

Andrew Nikitin and Petrovitch weren't just connected—they were brothers!

CHAPTER 13

JOE

MEETING FRIENDS IN THE STRANGEST OF PLACES

"And that's when I realized Petrovitch and Nikitin are brothers! It explains everything." Nancy called me as soon as her dinner with Jack Thorton ended, and told me she had crucial information. Frank and I were still conducting important investigations in the employee pool, but we raced to join her at the Courtyard Café, which was fast becoming our regular meet-up place.

Frank let out a low whistle. Nancy had really come through this time. Talk about zero to sixty in no time flat! After nearly a week of cleaning dishes and carrying guests' towels, this case had really gotten going. Once Nancy told us that Petrovitch and Nikitin were brothers, and that Nikitin was known to have money problems, we were pretty sure we had this case wrapped up.

Usually I could tell when people were lying, but Petrovitch had me completely convinced when he cautioned Frank and me against using violence. He was a good liar, as well as a good thief.

But not good enough. We had him, now we just had to reel him and his brother in. And for that, we needed hard evidence. I had an idea of where we were going to get it.

"I already searched his office and found nothing," I said. "Nikitin's got to have his share of the money somewhere. Even if he's sending most of it home, I'd guess he's keeping part of it. I think we need to search his room. Tonight."

"I agree," said Frank.

"Well, we're in luck," Nancy added. "I passed him in the lobby. He's working the front desk right now."

"All right, here's what we do." Nancy and Frank bent in to listen. "Nancy, he's definitely keeping an eye on you already. So you have to distract him. Keep him busy in the lobby, and if he leaves, call us and let us know. Frank and I are going to search his apartment."

"Where are Bess and George?" Frank asked. "I don't like the idea of you doing this alone, Nance."

Nance? Since when had Frank started calling Nancy by a pet name? I looked at him, and he blushed. That was my brother. Smooth as sandpaper.

"They're at the beach." Nancy said. "But I'll be in the

middle of a crowd. Nothing's going to happen to me. But, Joe—make sure your phone is on, okay?"

I flipped my phone out and turned the volume all the way up.

"There you go, *Nance*."

Frank kicked me under the table.

"Seriously, guys. Be careful. I've still got a bad feeling about all this. Something isn't quite right." Nancy looked worried.

"Don't worry. We'll be fine," I said. "We've got this case wrapped up."

Nancy left first, heading out to the lobby. We counted to one hundred, then followed her. By the time we got there, she had Nikitin deep in conversation, pouring over a map of the Wetlands. We scurried across the room and into the elevators without Nikitin ever once looking up at us.

We made it up to Nikitin's apartment. Unlike most of the other employees, he lived in the same building as the guests, since he was on call so often for emergencies. It must have made it all the easier for him to plan the robberies. We found his room and I pulled out my cell phone.

Have I mentioned my favorite part of being in ATAC? It's definitely the gadgets. Aside from making calls, our cell phones have dozens of special features you wouldn't find on even the latest iPhone.

I held the phone in front of the door's sensor pad. The light at the top of the phone strobed rapidly from red to green to blue and back. After a few seconds of this, I heard a click and Nikitin's door swung open.

"Jackpot! Age before beauty. Frank, after you." I held the door open.

Nikitin's apartment was pretty much the opposite of his office. There was stuff everywhere. Pictures on the walls, shelves filled with books, little tables with knick-knacks all over them. Wordlessly, Frank and I split up. We know how to search a room.

I worked my way along the left, Frank along the right. I flipped through the books on the shelves, but they all seemed real—no fake ones filled with money here.

"What is this?" I asked quietly. Even though the room was empty and we had Nancy as a lookout, it was standard procedure to be as subtle as possible when on a mission. The books were filled with weird script that looked positively medieval. I held one out to Frank.

"That's Cyrillic, the script Russian is written in. Didn't you do any research at all?

"Dude—it's summer. The only thing I'm researching is how to get the best tan once this mission is over."

Frank rolled his eyes and we went back to searching.

Everything in the room was, like, *really* Russian.

The art, the pictures, the books. He even had a set of those hollow dolls that have smaller versions of themselves inside them. I found a bunch of photos of a much younger Nikitin with a crowd of smaller kids around him. I could pick out Petrovitch in all of them too. I didn't see any photos of his parents, or of any older people at all, except one very old woman.

"Frank? You don't think these are all his siblings, do you?"

There were almost a dozen of them. No wonder Nikitin needed so much money to send back home. It didn't make the robberies right, but it did make me understand him a little better.

I flipped open the lid of a small wooden trunk, and there it all was—wallets, cell phones, jewelry, and a small pile of cash. If I'd had any doubts about Nikitin's being in on the crime, they were gone now.

"Frank, come here!"

Frank came running over. While he looked at what was in the trunk, I pulled out my phone and started snapping photos. Frank pulled a small notebook out of the trunk and flipped it open. Most of it was in Cyrillic, but there were columns of numbers that weren't hard to figure out—money borrowed, money sent, money owed. Frank took photos of it too.

Suddenly a noise came from behind the closed door at the other end of the room. Frank and I both froze.

Frank motioned for me to follow him and we crept quietly toward the door. Even if someone was there, I doubted they had heard us. It was probably just the air conditioning kicking on. Still, I picked up a small statue of a horse, just in case.

Frank looked back at me and shook his head. He motioned for me to put the statue down. He was right—our ATAC training always told us that bringing a weapon into an unknown situation just made it more likely that there would be violence, which was the last thing we wanted. But I made a mental note of where it was, just in case I needed it.

Frank pushed the door open and we moved in quickly. He went left, I went right. That way, if anyone was in the room, we'd have them flanked. But it didn't matter. Standing in the room were Petrovitch and Matthias!

Or rather, Matthias was standing in the room. Petrovitch was lying on the bed, tied up! His hands and feet were bound together with rope, and he wasn't struggling. I felt momentarily annoyed that Matthias had solved the case without us. If he'd involved us at all, we could totally have figured it out days ago! Then again, we didn't tell him what we were up to, so I guess I couldn't blame him.

"About time you guys got here," Matthias said. "I thought I was going to have to do all the work myself."

"What are you doing here?"

"I've been following Petrovitch all week. I caught him in the act of moving some of the stolen goods up here. I had no idea Andrew was involved. When I confronted Petrovitch, he attacked me. I just finished tying him up when you two burst in."

At the mention of his name, Petrovitch started struggling against the ropes. His motions seemed slow and uncoordinated. His eyes kept fluttering closed. It was almost like he had been drugged. He was pretty big; Matthias might have needed to give him something to keep him from getting loose. Still, it meant we needed to get him to a hospital soon. Sedatives and other drugs could really hurt someone if they weren't administered properly.

It was still hard for me to believe that Petrovitch had lied to us, but the evidence against him was pretty clear.

"Why didn't you tell us you were after him?" I didn't want to sound like a whiny kid, but we'd been wasting our time all week when we could have been working together.

"I knew he had a partner, and I was hoping the two of you would figure out who it was," Matthias answered. He seemed excited and amused, like there was some big inside joke. "And it seems like you have, eh?"

"Yeah," I said. "I overheard Nikitin talking on the

phone about 'laying low' and we figured out that he was in on something." I tried to explain everything we had learned without mentioning Nancy, but it was hard. Matthias didn't seem to care how we'd figured everything out though. He talked right over me as though I weren't even there.

"Now we just need to catch his brother. Are you guys ready for some action?"

"Yeah!" At least we'd be in on part of this case. Frank nodded his head cautiously.

"Okay, get ready." Matthias pointed to either side of the door, and Frank and I took up positions. Then he pulled out his cell phone.

"Andrew? Yes, it's Matthias. I was walking by your room, and I noticed the door was open. I think you should get up here immediately."

He hung up the phone and checked the knots on Petrovitch once again. Then he turned to us.

"We'll tackle him as soon as he comes in the door. Are you ready?"

We nodded. The room grew quiet as we all strained to hear the first signs of Nikitin entering the room. He was a big guy, but I had no doubt that, between the three of us, we could take him.

Da dun da dun dun dun!

My cell phone rang and I nearly jumped out of my skin.

"Shut that off!" Matthias hissed.

I looked at it guiltily. Nancy. Probably calling to tell us that Nikitin was on his way. I wanted to answer and explain what was happening, but Matthias looked like he was about to take it out of my hands and throw it against the wall, so I shut it off. I figured we'd have Nikitin in custody in ten minutes and the case wrapped up in an hour. I could call her later.

I had no idea how wrong I was.

CHAPTER **14**

NANCY

BESS GUESS

I was in luck. When I reached the concierge desk, Nikitin was standing there alone in front of a large computer, typing away. He looked distracted. I tried to steady my pounding heart and approached him.

"Hi!" I said, with a big plastic smile on my face. "How are you doing?"

"I am quite well, Ms. Drew," he said. "And yourself? I hope everything is living up to your expectations. Nothing wrong with your new accommodations, is there?"

I had to give it to him—Nikitin showed no sign that I was anything other than an ordinary guest. He was smooth.

"Oh no, the suite is lovely. Thank you so much."

"I am terribly sorry about what happened in your

old room. I assure you, it won't happen again."

I tried to think of something to say. The last thing I wanted to do was to get him talking about the break-ins. If he got suspicious, Frank and Joe could be in serious trouble. I wished Bess were here. She could talk to any guy, anywhere, about anything.

"I had dinner with Mr. Thorton earlier." It was the first thought to pop into my mind, so I went with it. "He told me you were from Russia."

"Yes. I moved to this country twelve years ago." He sighed and looked back at his computer screen. "I'm going to be shutting down the desk in a moment—is there anything I can help you with before I do?"

I was losing him. If his shift was ending, he could be heading up to his room at any moment. I had to get his attention and keep him down here. I tried again.

"I studied Russian history in school," I said quickly. "I've always been so interested in the country." I leaned over the desk, looking Nikitin directly in the eyes—a trick I'd seen Bess use many times before. He shifted toward me.

"Well, it is true. Russia has a fascinating history." Nikitin turned away from the computer and faced me directly. He was smiling now. Clearly, this was a topic that was close to his heart.

"Uh-huh," I said, smiling at him again. That was all the encouragement Nikitin needed.

"For instance, did you know that Empress Yekaterina—Catherine the Great, you might know her as—ruled Russia for thirty-four years? She was one of the most powerful women of her time. There is a reason Russia is known as the 'motherland.'"

This was going to be easy. I barely had to say anything. So long as I kept nodding my head, Nikitin kept talking. And he was right—it *was* fascinating. Despite what I'd told him, I didn't know anything about Russian history. When I got back home, I'd have to get some books from the library. Any place with a history of strong women was a place I wanted to read about!

I figured another fifteen minutes and Frank and Joe would be safely out of Nikitin's room. There was a large clock on the wall behind him, and I watched the minutes tick down. It was after nine, and the lobby was nearly empty. Somewhere in the back of my mind, I noticed two pairs of footsteps running toward me, but I didn't think anything of them until a hand grabbed my shoulder.

"Nancy!" I spun around. Bess and George were standing behind me. "We've been trying to call you!"

It wasn't like Bess to interrupt a conversation. She looked upset and flustered. Her cheeks were red, and both she and George were sweating. If I hadn't known any better, I would have guessed that they ran all the way from the beach to the hotel.

"I'm sorry, Bess. I must have put my phone in my purse and not noticed it because I was *talking to Andrew*." I tried to emphasize those last words. I couldn't afford to lose Nikitin's attention right now.

"I'm sorry," Bess said, leaning over my shoulder to talk to Nikitin. "Do you mind if we borrow Nancy for a minute?"

Before Nikitin had a chance to say anything, Bess and George had literally pulled me away from the desk. I'd never seen them act like this before! Something must be going on. Still, I was working with Frank and Joe, and I couldn't let them down.

"Guys, I can't. I have to keep Nikitin occupied." I pulled free of their hands, but when I looked back, Nikitin had already left the desk and the computer was shut off. I looked around the lobby and spotted him heading for the elevators. I was too late.

"Nancy." George looked me dead in the eye. "We need to talk to you. It's important."

I knew from the way she said it that it was true. They needed me now. They were my friends, and I trusted their intuition. If Bess and George thought that something was important, so did I. Besides, there was nothing I could do about Nikitin now.

"Okay. Let me just warn Frank and Joe."

I called Joe, but it rang twice and went to his voice mail. I just hoped they were out of the room already.

If not . . . I couldn't think about what would happen if Nikitin caught them in his room. He was huge, bigger than Frank and Joe combined, and if he surprised them, they'd be in trouble. I left Joe a message saying Nikitin was on his way, and to call me if they needed backup.

"What's going on?" I asked Bess and George.

"It'll be easier to show you than to explain. Let's go to the room."

We headed upstairs in silence. I couldn't help worrying about Frank and Joe, even though I knew they could take care of themselves. Still, I felt like I had let them down.

When we got to the room, Bess went straight for the listening device we'd found in the couch. She tore it out of the fabric and tossed it out the window.

"There, now we can really talk," she said. She sat down on the couch, obviously waiting for something. I joined her.

George went to her room and brought out a small black bag I hadn't seen before. It looked heavy. Where had it come from? What was going on? I waited.

"Remember when I went out to the swamp with Matthias?" George asked.

I nodded.

"Well, he gave me more than just a tour. He gave me a necklace. I didn't think much about it at the time. I thought it was a silly piece of costume jewelry. I should have said something sooner, but I didn't want you guys to make too much of it."

George looked embarrassed. She handed the bag to Bess.

"Oh, George," I said. "We wouldn't make fun of you! It's great that Matthias likes you."

Even if he is a creep, I thought.

"No, Nancy. That's not it," she said.

Bess opened the bag and poured the contents out into her hands. The necklace was made of three thick strands of golden metal braided together, with cut red glass studded all around. It glittered in the light. For a piece of plastic, it looked beautiful. But I still didn't understand why they needed to talk to me right now.

Bess looked at me expectantly. I shrugged. What did she want me to say?

"Don't you recognize it?" she asked.

I shook my head no.

"Argh! The two of you. George didn't either. This is Jasmina's necklace—it's worth millions!"

Speechless, I took the necklace from Bess's hands. It was heavy, the way real gold should be. And if it was real gold, then it wasn't studded with cut glass. They were rubies, a dozen huge rubies.

"Are you sure it's the same one, not a replica?" I asked.

"Let's check," said George. She grabbed her laptop off the coffee table and started it up. Within a few seconds, she had pulled up a picture of Jasmina. We compared the necklace in my hands with the one she was wearing in the photo. There was no question. It was the same one!

"But . . . how did *Matthias* get this?" I asked out loud, already knowing the answer. Matthias was behind the break-ins.

"I should have known it wasn't just plastic! I'm sorry, Nancy, this is all my fault." George was nearly crying. I hugged her.

"This isn't your fault, George. Matthias had us all fooled. Including Frank and Joe. If you hadn't gotten to know him, we probably never would have caught on."

I tried to comfort her, but George was pretty upset at herself. I hugged her close. Things started falling into place in my mind. Matthias must have known that Frank and Joe were in ATAC. That's why he'd been trying to kill them when I first saw them in the swamp. And he must have been the one who searched our suite. He probably thought that *we* were in ATAC as well, since we knew Frank and Joe. When he couldn't find anything that tied us to ATAC, he bugged our new room to make sure. He had rigged the balcony to collapse, knowing that Frank and Joe would be looking for evidence. I bet he had been listening in on them as well. He probably knew everything.

I got a sick feeling in the pit of my stomach. Frank and Joe were in terrible danger, and they had no idea. Frantically, I called Joe.

No answer.

15

FRANK

BETRAYED!

I don't know how long we stood in the dark, waiting for Nikitin to show up. The minutes before a fight always seem to stretch on forever. I could hear Joe and Matthias breathing near me. I could feel the adrenaline pumping through my veins. I was glad we were finally nearing the end of this case.

I heard the front door of the apartment open. My heart started beating harder, and I crouched down, getting ready to cut off Nikitin's exit as soon as he walked into the bedroom.

"Matthias?" He called out.

"In here!"

Matthias looked at me and Joe. We nodded.

Everyone was in position. In a moment, this would all be over.

Nikitin opened the door and went in a few steps before he noticed Matthias. He stopped dead in his tracks, and I slipped behind him to cut off his escape. We had him trapped now. Nikitin swung his head wildly, noticing me and Joe.

"What's going on?" he yelled. "Matthias?"

Joe was approaching him slowly from the left.

"Give yourself up now, Nikitin. We have all the evidence we need. We know you're the one behind the break-ins." Joe was talking quietly, trying to calm Nikitin down and keep his attention.

"I thought we had a deal," Nikitin said, looking at Matthias.

Matthias said nothing, but he stepped toward Nikitin with his hands in fists, moving away from the bed. Nikitin started to take a step back, when suddenly he caught sight of Petrovitch, still tied up.

"Petrovitch!" he yelled and surged forward, knocking Matthias out of the way with one arm. He tossed him aside like he was made out of tissue paper. Matthias landed hard, all the air leaving his lungs in a sharp *whoof!*

Everything was moving too fast for me to follow. What did Nikitin mean by "a deal"? Something was wrong, but I didn't have the time to figure it out.

Nikitin leaned over the bed and started trying to

untie Petrovitch. Joe leaped onto his back and grabbed Nikitin by the head. Nikitin reared up and shook. I tried to find a safe way to tackle him, but Joe was flying every which way and I was afraid I was just as likely to hurt him as Nikitin. Joe held on for a second, but Nikitin broke his hold and sent him flying across the room too. He landed in a heap, but he seemed to be okay. He was on his feet again a second later.

Matthias was getting up, and Joe wasn't out of the fight either. Nikitin looked around the room and realized there was no way he was going to win. Then he looked at me, the only thing standing between him and the door. I braced myself as he charged.

It was like trying to stop a train. He ran right through me as though I wasn't there. I blasted into the air, my entire chest filled with pain. I was going to be one big bruise in the morning. But our ATAC training had served me well. Even as I was tumbling through the air, I managed to snag one arm around Nikitin's throat. With the other one, I grabbed the door frame.

Nikitin went down like a tree, falling backward. My arm was nearly ripped out of its socket, but I managed to hold on. I leapt on top of him, hoping to pin him down for the crucial moment it would take Joe and Matthias to get out here and help me.

We rolled over and over, knocking into tables and chairs. We were so close, it was hard to hit each other.

Nikitin managed to get his arms around me, and I could feel him squeezing the air out of my lungs. I flipped around wildly, trying to break free, but his arms were like two steel coils.

I spotted the horse statue Joe had picked up earlier on the floor near us. I grabbed it and hit Nikitin as hard as I could across the head. It was a bad angle, so it was only a slight blow, but it was enough to take him by surprise and make him let go momentarily. I slipped out of his grasp and struggled to my feet.

Nikitin was on all fours, shaking his head and trying to get up. I put him in a sleeper hold, cutting off the blood to his brain. He tried to fight me, but soon he sank to the floor and fell unconscious.

"Matthias! Joe! Call hotel security—Nikitin's going to need an ambulance!" I checked his pulse. It was strong. He was out, but not in any danger, though he was bleeding from where I hit him. I wasn't surprised. He was built like an ox. Hopefully he'd be out long enough for the police to get him in handcuffs.

Where were Matthias and Joe? I hoped they hadn't been hit harder than I thought. I ran back into the bedroom.

Joe was on the floor, unconscious. *That's strange*, I thought. He was getting to his feet when I last saw him. Nikitin must have given him a concussion. We'd need to get him to the hospital as well. But where was Matthias?

I felt a sharp prick at the back of my neck. I turned around and Matthias was standing there holding a needle.

"What the heck?" I said. Or at least, that's what I tried to say. My tongue was heavy and I couldn't move my mouth properly. I tried to walk, but my legs gave out beneath me. I landed in a heap on top of Joe.

I heard Matthias laughing above me. I tried to get the cell phone out of Joe's pocket to call Nancy for help, but I could barely move.

"Look at the perfect Hardys now. The golden boys of ATAC. Hope you're ready for an early retirement."

Everything went black.

RACE AGAINST TIME

I dialed Joe again. And again. Nothing. It went straight to voice mail every time. The feeling in my stomach became heavier, like a brick sinking into a lake. Joe and Frank were in trouble.

"George, can you find a detailed map of the Wetlands? We need to find out where Nikitin's and Matthias's rooms are."

"Sure, Nancy." George started typing away on the keyboard, her hands flying over the keys. She sniffed a few times, but she'd mostly stopped crying.

I placed the necklace back in the black velvet bag and hid it under one of the couches. Hopefully, Matthias wouldn't come back to look for it. If he tore the place apart again, he'd find it. But if he had the chance to search our rooms, it probably didn't matter anymore whether he found the necklace. At least not for us.

Bess and I sat silently, our hands clenched, while we waited for George to find the information we needed. As the seconds ticked past, I could feel the tension mounting. What if Nikitin had overpowered Frank and Joe? What if they were on their way to Matthias's room right now? What if, what if, what if.

"Got it, Nancy," George said finally. "Nikitin is in this building, Room four-seven-one. Matthias is over in the employee area. Bungalow 8, Room 7."

"George, you're incredible!" Bess jumped with joy. If it had a chip in it, George could make it work.

"All right, let's head to Nikitin's room first. Hopefully we'll find them there."

We tore out of the suite and over to the elevator area. Everything seemed to be moving so slowly. The elevator, my feet. Everything, that is, except for time, which was flying by. Every second, I imagined Frank and Joe in danger. I kept remembering Matthias with the paddle raised over his head, ready to kill them. What if this time I didn't make it in time?

But I couldn't think that way. It would drive me crazy. Frank and Joe were safe. I just had to find them.

When the doors finally opened on the fourth floor, we took off running down the hallway. We hadn't gone ten feet before I tried to dodge around a room service cart and tripped and fell.

"Stupid high heels!" I yanked them off my feet and threw them across the hall.

"You know, one day, Nancy, you're really going to have to learn how to run in heels." Bess kicked her feet up at me to show the dainty high-heeled sandals she was wearing. They were cute—but not the best footwear for a mission.

Within a few seconds, we were running again. I felt much better in bare feet. We found Nikitin's room. The door was open.

"Hello?" I called through the door. "Frank? Joe?"

Silence was the only answer.

Inside, the room was a mess. Furniture had been overturned and books strewn across the floor. I had an eerie feeling of déjà vu, remembering back to our first suite. The cleaning staff at the Wetlands must be kept pretty busy. We split up to search the room, looking for anything that might indicate where the boys were now.

"Oh no!" Bess cried out suddenly.

"What is it?" George and I rushed over to her side, and then stopped. On the floor in front of her was a small puddle of blood, smeared around the carpet as though someone had rolled in it.

"There's not a lot of blood. There'd be more if . . ."

I didn't want to finish the sentence. I bent down to examine the blood, trying to keep myself from panicking. *Breath, Nancy,* I told myself. *You can't help them if you can't think clearly.*

"It's still wet. Whatever happened here, it was recent."

We crept into the bedroom and found more of the same. Mess, everywhere. It was clear there'd been a huge fight of some kind. But there was no sign of Frank or Joe. Or Nikitin, for that matter. Thankfully, there was no more blood either.

On the floor behind the bed I found a needle. I picked it up carefully, making certain not to touch the sharp end.

"What's that?" Bess asked.

"No way to know for certain, but I'd bet it contained some sort of sedative." I pulled out an old plastic container from my purse. It had once been Hannah's eyeglass case, but now I used it to hold evidence when I was on a case. Particularly sharp, possibly poisonous evidence.

I inhaled deeply, trying to stay focused and calm. I doubted that Frank and Joe would have drugged Nikitin.

We checked the closets, kitchen, and bathroom quickly, but came up with nothing. Frank and Joe had been here, but they were gone now, with no sign of where they were headed or if they had gone on their own two feet or been dragged.

"There's nothing else here," I said. "George, can you lead us to Matthias's room?"

George nodded and we took off. I was careful to leave the door just barely cracked open—not enough that anyone would notice, but enough so that we could get back in if we needed to. I walked carefully past the room service cart this time. Then an idea hit me.

I flipped up the white tablecloth. It was dark underneath, so I pulled my flashlight from my purse. I always carry one, just in case. Sure enough, when I turned on the light, I could see small drops of blood on the undercarriage of the cart.

"Someone used this cart to carry the body—or bodies—out of the room and into the elevator," I said. But why didn't they take the cart? They must have been bringing them somewhere directly off the elevator . . . but where?

Bess made a strangled noise at the word "body," and we all tried not to think about what it implied.

George led the way out of the main part of the hotel and over to the employee area. I had never been over there before, and I was glad it was dark so that no one stopped and asked to see our ID badges.

After a few wrong turns, we ended up at a low bungalow, painted a tropical turquoise. We circled around it, looking for Room 7. It was the last one, and the door was right up against the wall that went around the outside of the resort. There was a window to one side, a streetlight above, and (unfortunately) a sensor pad.

If it was a regular lock, I could have picked it. That was one of the tricks of the trade I had learned over the last few years of detective work. But I didn't even know how these sensors worked, let alone how to disable one.

Bess knocked but got no answer. There were no lights on inside, and it sounded quiet. Then she tried the door, hoping it might be unlocked. No luck.

"I think we're going to have to do this the old-fashioned way," I said. "George, can you get the light?"

George reached up and unscrewed the light on the side of the building. The alley was plunged into darkness. I unzipped my purse and poured everything out onto the ground. Then I put my elbow inside it, as though it were an elbow guard. I glanced back at the front of the alley, to make sure no one was looking. Bess casually strolled in front of me, hiding me from view.

Crash!

The glass of the windowpane shattered as I slammed my elbow through it. The purse protected me from getting cut. I used it to knock away the sharp shards of glass left in the frame. Then I reached in and turned the doorknob from inside, while George picked up the stuff from my purse and handed it to me.

"Housekeeping!" Bess called out as we walked in. I stifled a laugh.

Inside, the room was nearly the opposite of Nikitin's. It was sparsely decorated, with nothing on the walls, no books on the shelves, and very few personal effects anywhere. In one corner was a very large television. It was spotlessly clean. *At least,* I thought to myself, *that makes it easy to search.*

"Bess, you take the kitchen. George, the bedroom. I'll look in here."

I checked under the chairs and couches, but there was nothing. Remembering the hidden listening device in our suite, I felt around for strange lumps in the cushions, but came up empty.

"Bingo!" Bess called out. She walked back into the living room holding a large container marked FLOUR.

"Evidence that he likes to bake?" I asked.

"Or that he likes dough," she said. She angled the can toward me. It was filled with cash, wallets, watches, and jewelry.

"Take some photos of all that. I'm going to keep searching."

I looked around the room. Something wasn't right. Then it hit me. The television was angled away from everything else. None of the chairs faced it. It would be impossible to watch anything on it. Who has a television that large that they can't watch?

I looked at it closely. There were little scratch marks around the frame, and all the screws had been removed. It looked as though it had been hollowed out.

Sure enough, the glass on the front popped out easily when I pulled on it. Inside was a large cache of papers, photos, and DVDs. Everything had the ATAC logo on it. At the bottom of the pile was an ID card that identified Matthias as a member of ATAC!

Could I have been wrong? Was Matthias working with Frank and Joe? Something didn't add up. I flipped through the papers, looking at descriptions of old missions and various materials. Some of them looked different from the others, cruder, less polished. Most were addressed to Matthias, but a few had Frank's and Joe's names on them. There were also tons of photos, mostly of Frank and Joe, which seemed to have been taken by someone in hiding, using a telephoto lens.

I laid the papers on the ground and stared at them. Matthias definitely had the stolen goods from the robberies. And he hadn't mentioned anything to Frank or Joe about it. But he also seemed to be in with ATAC. I tried to piece together what it could all mean. Then it came to me.

What if Matthias was just pretending to be an ATAC agent?

Some of these papers were real ATAC missions, but some of them looked fake. Homemade. Maybe Matthias had made up this mission and committed all the robberies just to lead Frank and Joe down here. If that was the case, they were in even more danger than I had ever realized. From the pictures, it looked as though he had been following them for a long time. The sick feeling in my stomach grew worse. This whole thing had been a trap from the very beginning.

"Nancy, Bess! Come in here," George yelled from the bedroom. I stuffed the papers into my purse and ran to join her.

The bedroom was nearly as empty as the living room—a bed, a desk with a chair, a lamp, and a chest of drawers. George had clearly already opened all the drawers and checked under the mattress—they were a mess. George was sitting at the desk, which was pressed up against one wall. It was an old-fashioned rolltop, and unlike in every other part of the apartment, its surface was cluttered with stuff.

I peered over George's shoulder. In front of her was a large machine that looked like a radio from an old movie. There was a huge pair of headphones connected to it, like the kind that DJs wore to block out all the other sound in a club. There was also a stack of blank staff ID cards on the table, as well as some tiny electronics and gadgets that I couldn't identify.

"What is all this stuff?" I asked George.

"These," she said, holding up a handful of the small electronics, "are tiny listening devices. And this"—she pointed to the radio—"is the receiver."

George held up a tiny gun-shaped object.

"Matthias used this soldering iron to place the listening devices inside these staff IDs. See?"

George pointed back to one of the dials on the radio. It looked like a regular station tuner, except instead of normal markings, it had only three, which had been handwritten on Post-it notes and stuck to the machine. One was labeled *Joe*, the other *Frank*, and the third, *Nancy*.

So this was why Matthias had been so crazy about Joe and Frank wearing their IDs! An idea came to me.

"If Matthias used this to spy on Frank and Joe, and now he has them with him, maybe we can use it to find them."

I picked up the headset and put it on. George flipped the power switch and turned the dial to the place marked *Joe*. I listened for a second, but there was no sound. Either Joe didn't have his ID on him . . . or he wasn't making any noise.

"Nothing," I said. George turned it to Frank.

This time I heard something. A rushing *whooshing* sound, like wind. I couldn't tell what it was.

"There's something, but I don't know what."

Bess took the headphones from me and listened for a second. Then she shook her head.

"I can't make it out either," she said.

She handed the headphones to George. As soon as she put them on, her eyes grew wide with recognition.

"I know that sound!" she yelled. "It's one of the hover boats. They're in the swamps! And I bet I know exactly where Matthias is taking them."

CHAPTER 17

JOE

ALL TIED UP

I woke up from the strangest dream. In it, I was a little kid, and my dad was carrying me to bed. But my bed was one of those carts you use to move food in a restaurant, and my dad was Matthias Dunstock. Nightmare!

I shook my head to try and clear the dream from my mind and wake up. That was a bad idea. The slightest motion made my stomach feel queasy. My head was pounding, a rhythmic pain that surged through my brain every time my heart beat. I opened my eyes for a second, but everything was blurry and indistinct. Having my eyes open made my stomach feel even worse, and I couldn't make out anything anyway, so I shut them again quickly.

The one glance I had of my surroundings, though

too quick and confused to tell me where I was, did tell me where I wasn't. I wasn't at home in my room. In fact, I didn't think I was in a room at all. Wherever I was, I was lying on the ground in a heap. There were all sorts of things under me, pressing up against me. I tried to move my arms and prop myself up, but I couldn't. At first I thought they had fallen asleep, then I thought they were pinned behind me by whatever I was lying against, but as I struggled to move, I realized they were tied. Adrenaline surged through me as I realized that, wherever I was, I was in danger.

I tried to think. I could feel a breeze blowing, so I had to be in motion. Was I in a car? No . . . it didn't feel like a car. We were bouncing more than a car would. A train? No, the engine didn't sound right for a train, and besides, I wouldn't be out in the open on a train. Then I had it! A boat. I was in some sort of boat.

I couldn't remember how I'd gotten there. The last thing I remembered clearly was talking to Nancy and Frank. I remembered heading up to Nikitin's apartment . . . but everything after that was fuzzy. Matthias had been there. And Petrovitch?

Suddenly, I remembered.

Nikitin had thrown me off him and I landed in a heap in the corner of his bedroom. Just as I was getting up, he ran right through Frank and out the door. I was about to run out and help Frank, when Matthias called my name. I turned back toward him, and I felt a sharp stab in my arm. I fell to my knees, and Matthias was standing over me with a needle. Then I blacked out.

The pain in my head was starting to die down. The fight-or-flight reaction was kicking in, and my body was becoming more responsive. Tentatively, I opened my eyes again. Frank was tied up to my left, his head rolled back against the side of the boat. I would have thought he was sleeping, except for the fact that, for once in his life, he wasn't snoring like a buzzsaw.

"Frank!" I hissed, hoping he was just pretending to be unconscious. He didn't move. Long after I knew he was out of it, I continued to stare at him, hoping he would wake up. But he was down for the count.

I looked to my right. Nikitin was slumped there, tied up as well. Blood was slowly dripping from his forehead, and his skin was a pale color. His breathing was shallow. He didn't look good. If I craned my head, I could see Matthias beyond him, standing at the head of the boat, piloting it.

What was Matthias doing? He was an ATAC agent! Why had he drugged us?

My blood froze in my veins as I realized . . . he'd gone rogue! It was almost unimaginable, a fellow agent turned criminal. It was terrifying. He had the resources and training of ATAC behind him. Who knew what he could do. He could be incredibly dangerous . . . as Frank and I had already discovered, too late.

Matthias didn't seem to have noticed that I was awake. At least that was one thing in my favor. The element of surprise. Not that I could do much with it right now.

It was dark, but I could just make out the edges of the swamp around us. I had no idea how long I'd been out for. We could be halfway to Cuba by now!

If Frank and Nikitin were to either side of me, then the body I was lying against had to be Petrovitch. I wondered what his role was in all of this. Nikitin had seemed surprised to see him tied up on the bed. Were the two brothers involved in the robberies at all? Was this all Matthias's scheme? And why was he doing it? So many questions, and no time to get answers.

My fingers were stiff from being tied behind my back, but I started to feel around to get a sense of how I was bound. Rope, not too thick. The thicker the rope was, the easier it was to untie. This stuff would be difficult. I tested it, pulling this way and that, but the knots were good. Of course they were. They were the ones ATAC had trained us to use.

Because it was thin, though, the rope would be easy to wear through, if I could find something sharp to rub against. I felt around behind me, but Petrovitch was so large, I couldn't reach the edges of the boat around him. I hoped the noise of the boat's engine would keep Matthias from noticing that I was awake.

My moving around must have tipped off Petrovitch to the fact that I was awake. I felt a slight movement from him too. His fingers grasped mine, squeezed them once, and then released. He was trying to send me a message! But could I trust him?

Matthias cut the engine all at once, and everything flew forward. I slammed my head into Nikitin, but he was like a giant mannequin and didn't even move. My face was stuck in his side, and I could barely breath. I struggled to right myself. I didn't live through all my ATAC missions just to be smothered in the armpit of an unconscious giant!

I felt a sharp pain in the back of my head. A hand wrapped around my hair and pulled me upright.

"I'm so glad you're awake," Matthias said. "I was afraid I was going to have to kill you in your sleep. And that wouldn't be anywhere near as much fun."

He shoved me backward, and I fell hard against someone again. Frank or Petrovitch, I couldn't tell for sure. Whoever it was didn't move.

"You're not going to get away with this," I said. "ATAC knows where we are. Even if you kill us, they'll find you."

Matthias laughed.

"ATAC has no idea you're down here. Your whole

mission was a fake. Do you think it was just chance that brought you down here? I guess the great Hardys aren't as smart as everyone says."

Matthias's voice had a mean, hard edge to it, but also a whiny one, like a bratty kid boasting about his grades. I couldn't believe he'd faked the whole thing. What possible reason could he have? I could understand his wanting to kill us because we were on to his scheme, but why bring us down here in the first place?

ATAC had trained us for hostage situations. And one of the first things they said was to keep your captor talking. So long as they were interested in communicating, they weren't ready to kill you. I had to keep Matthias occupied until I could free myself. Or until Nancy could find us.

"Why?" I asked. "Why lure us down here where we could discover your robbery scheme? Why not just take the money and run?"

"You think this is about the robberies? This had nothing to do with money! It was always about you. You and your brother. The *golden boys* of ATAC. Just because your father started the agency, everyone thinks you're the best."

Matthias was angry now, talking fast and low. He leaned in close to my face and grabbed me by the hair again.

"You."

Slap!

"Aren't."

Slap!

"Anything."

Slap!

"Special."

My head was ringing by the time he let me go. He had some arm on him.

"Okay!" I said. "I'll tell you everything. Just stop! Your breath is killing me."

Matthias's face turned into a mask of rage, and I thought for a moment I had pushed him too far. Then he just laughed and sat back down.

"You always have a joke ready, don't you? I've been following you for months, you and your brother, learning everything about you. You'd have been dead days ago if that friend of yours hadn't gotten in the way. So cute—she fancies herself a detective. She's dumber than the two of you."

Matthias turned away from me and started pulling things out of a bag at his feet. I saw more needles, a glass bottle full of clear liquid, and a gun. I tried to think of something else to keep him talking.

"And these two? Were they involved at all?" I nodded my head at Petrovitch and Nikitin.

Matthias smiled, a sick, twisted smile.

"Oh, you wouldn't believe how easy my friend Nikitin

here was to manipulate. Money, money, money. 'My family,'" he whined all the time. "'They need help.'"

Matthias pushed Nikitin over with his foot. He slumped to the floor of the boat, blood leaking faster from his head now. I took advantage of his momentary distraction to lean back, my fingers stretching out behind me. Quickly, I found what I was looking for— another knot. I began to untie it as Matthias started talking again. I hoped whoever I was freeing was conscious . . . and on my side.

"His dumb ox of a brother I would have let live. I don't understand how someone can be so large and yet have a brain so small. He almost told you that I was the last one in Jasmina's room, you know. Thankfully, I was listening to the two of you and was able to arrange an 'emergency massage' to call him away. But then he came across me moving the last of the stolen stuff to Nikitin's room, and I was forced to knock him out. Luckily, four bodies are just as easy to dump as three."

I almost had it. I could feel the knots coming apart beneath my fingers. I just needed Matthias to keep talking for another few minutes. He leaned in close to me again, his stinking breath in my face.

"This is one of my favorite spots in the swamp. So private. Do you like it? George certainly did. Maybe, after you've gone missing, I can take her out here to console her. We can have a picnic . . . over your dead bodies."

Matthias pulled back suddenly. "What is that?"

I had no idea what he was talking about. I looked around, trying to figure out what he was seeing. Then I realized it wasn't something he saw, it was something he heard. The whine of another hover boat, cutting through the air.

Someone was coming. And I was pretty sure her name was Nancy Drew.

NANCY TO THE RESCUE

We must have run the entire way from Matthias's apartment to the entrance of the hotel proper. We flew past a few startled guests, yelling, "I'm sorry!" and, "Excuse me!" every couple of feet. Who knew how much time Frank and Joe had left. There wasn't a moment to spare.

There was a dock for the hover boats right underneath the hotel. The main elevators would take you down there. Matthias must have knocked out Frank and Joe somehow, and then carried them out on the room service cart and dumped them into the elevator. From there, it was just down a few flights and they were home free. I had to hand it to Matthias, it was a brilliant way to get them out of the hotel without anyone seeing.

The dock itself was surrounded by a high fence designed to keep people out after hours. There we found more proof that Frank and Joe had definitely been that way: the lock on the gate had been picked and left open, and there were scraps of fabric caught in the sharp edges of the chicken wire at a low height, as though someone had been dragged through the gate.

There were three boats sitting in the dock, their giant fans still. Hover boats skirt the top of the water, unlike conventional boats, which sit in it. The fans are their main method of moving forward. Regular boats don't work in the swamp because the water is so shallow, a conventional boat motor can shatter its blades on the ground.

"George, do you know where the keys are kept?" I asked, as we looked around the space.

"No! When I came here before, the keys were just in the ignitions of all the boats."

They must have taken them away to prevent unauthorized people from using them. George and I started searching the small office to the left of the dock, but there was nothing to be found. Then we heard the roar of an engine and the whirr of a fan. We came running back out.

"Bess? You found the keys?" I yelled.

"Who needs keys when you have a set of pliers?" Bess held up some tools she had picked up off the floor of the dock. Behind her, I could see the wires sticking out of the dashboard. She'd taken the ignition apart and hot-wired the boat! She's a genius with machines—though we were going to have to explain that later to Mr. Thorton. But knowing Bess, she'd be able to put it back together just as easily as she took it apart.

In a few seconds, we were off, zooming through the swamp. It was already dark out, and once we got away from the lights of the hotel, it was hard to see more than a few feet in front of us. Bess flipped a few switches, and two giant floodlights turned on. They were so bright, you could feel the heat coming off them, like spotlights at a theater. They cut two narrow channels through the darkness, but everything else was black as tar.

The swamp at night was a terrifying place. Strange noises came from all sides, high-pitched wailing bird calls, splashing, and creaking. Wet strands of Spanish moss, like cobwebs, only thicker and green, reached down from the trees and caught on our faces and hair. George directed, Bess drove, and I stared off into the night, straining my eyes to catch a glimpse of Frank, Joe, or Matthias.

"I think it's a left up ahead," George muttered. "No, a right. Oh, Nancy, I don't know if I can remember the right way!"

George kicked the front of the boat, hard, her frustration driving her crazy. I reached out and put my arm around her shoulder.

"You can do this, George."

"Okay. Okay. Go . . . right."

We stood in silence at the front of the boat, like the carved prow of an old pirate ship. How easily everything could fall apart. If we were going the wrong way. If they weren't in the swamp at all. If Matthias had already hurt them. If, if, if. I couldn't stop thinking about it.

"There!"

It was George who finally spotted them by the glint of our lights off their boat. It was just sitting there silently. Bess turned the wheel slightly, never slowing down, putting their boat directly in our floodlights. We were headed right toward them, but I still couldn't see anyone on the boat. Were we too late already?

Suddenly, Matthias reared up into the light. He looked insane, his hair wild, his face red and twisted with anger. He might have been screaming, but I couldn't hear him over the roar of our engine. We were so close to him, I could see the wind ruffling his hair.

He put his hand into the waist of his pants, and I knew from the angle of his wrist and the way he moved, he could only be reaching for a gun.

"What do I do?" Bess yelled. Matthias had pulled out a pistol and was aiming it right for us. I looked over at Bess, about to tell her to turn the wheel and get us out of his line of sight, when I realized that was exactly what Matthias would be expecting. Instead, I leaned over and shoved the throttle down.

If we'd been going fast before, now we were racing like a Nascar driver, skipping along the surface of the water. Matthias barely had time to react before our boat collided with his and everyone was sent flying.

Petrovitch somersaulted through the air like a giant rag doll, and then slammed to the ground on the island where the boat had been tied up.

I managed to hold on to the dashboard of our boat, and struggled to stay on my feet. George and Bess both fell to the floor beside me. Matthias's boat was cracked in the collision, and quickly began to sink. But where were Frank and Joe? And where was Matthias and, more important, his gun?

"Nancy!" I heard Joe's voice coming from the bottom of the hover boat. I peered down and saw Joe, Frank, and Nikitin all tied up. There was at least an inch of water around their feet, and more was pouring in every minute. I rushed down to untie them, George and Bess following right behind me.

Frank was barely conscious, and I ran to untie him first. The knots were slippery from the water and tied tightly. In the dark, it was hard to see the rope to untie it, and fear made my fingers awkward and clumsy.

Between the two of us, Bess and I managed to get Frank's legs untied.

From beneath the dark water, Matthias suddenly emerged. Clenched in his hands was the gun, which was pointing directly at my chest.

"Why, Ms. Drew," he said. "We simply have to stop meeting like this. Thankfully, I know just how to ensure you never get in my way again."

Time seemed to freeze. In a few seconds, Matthias would shoot me. Then he would shoot George and Bess, and leave Frank, Joe, and Nikitin to drown. No one would ever know what had happened to us.

Matthias cocked the trigger, and I looked for something to throw at him, some way to distract him, something—anything—to prevent the inevitable. Then a roar came from the dark of the swamp, and a piece of the island seemed to detach itself and come rushing out of the night. For a second, it hung in the air, a darker piece of darkness, and then it landed on Matthias. It was Petrovitch!

I didn't see what happened after Petrovitch jumped on Matthias.

I heard sounds of fighting: punches landing, water splashing, the occasional grunt of pain. I was too busy pulling the ropes off Joe and Frank. We managed to get them free just in time.

Right as we helped Frank half-consciously stumble

onto the safety of the island, the hover boat gave a tortured *crack*! and split in two. Both sides quickly sank beneath the surface.

Petrovitch had Matthias pinned to the ground. He was struggling weakly beneath Petrovitch, but he was no match for his giant strength. Petrovitch looked up as the boat disappeared into the swamp.

"Androvitch? My brother! Where is he?"

I looked around the island. There was no sign of him anywhere. Without a word, Joe leapt into the water.

Long seconds passed. The darkness and the silence grew. An occasional bubble of air drifted up to the surface of the swamp, but aside from that, everything was still.

The water rippled where Joe had dived in, concentric circles which grew bigger and bigger as they expanded outward from the point of impact. Then those too stopped, and there was nothing, no movement, no sound, no sign of Joe or Nikitin. I realized I was holding my breath.

Joe's head broke the water like a fist through a glass window. Sprays of water went everywhere. He gasped loudly, sucking air into his desperate lungs. Then he slowly raised his arms out of the swamp, dragging the limp—but still breathing—figure of Androvitch Nikitin out of the water. They were both alive!

CHAPTER 19

FRANK

SURF'S UP!

"Help!" Joe screamed. He was cornered.

George came running through the water, Bess right behind her. Joe dodged to the right and left them in his wake. I was in the clear. Joe threw the beach ball to me—and Nancy snagged it out of the air. I tackled her. She went down like a ton of bricks.

I had the ball in my hand, but Bess leaped onto my back before I got more than two feet. Then Joe was on top of her, and George on top of him. Soon we were all in a pile in the shallow water. When we finally came up for air, the ball was floating five feet away.

"I think the ball is laughing at us," Nancy said.

"It's just intimidated by my natural athletic ability," Joe said, winking at Bess.

George came up behind him and easily dunked him underwater.

"Your natural what?" she said.

We all headed back to our beach chairs, our game forgotten. Now that our mission was over, we still had a day to enjoy the sun. With Petrovitch's muscle and Bess's know-how, we'd managed to get one of the hover boats up and running that night in the swamp.

I came to shortly after Joe pulled Nikitin out of the water. His skin was white and clammy, and the blood from his forehead had caked on his face. Mixed with the mud from the bottom of the swamp, it made him look like an extra from a zombie film. Thankfully, I knew some first aid and was able to stop the bleeding and get him bandaged up. We rushed him back to the hotel— along with a seriously angry Matthias Dunstock.

I was still shocked that the whole thing had been a lie. I called Dad right after we got Matthias and Nikitin in custody, and he'd had no idea we thought we were on a mission. He believed our story about the essay competition—no wonder he'd seemed so good at "acting" surprised. He really had been surprised! As for Matthias, he remembered him as a good kid, and a brilliant agent, but a highly competitive one. In the end, his competitive side won out over his better nature. ATAC was taking him into special custody to try and rehabilitate him, but who knew what would happen.

The sun was setting, and Joe, George, and Thatcher were dragging over big logs to start a fire and barbecue. Katlyn and Thatcher were good friends, and he'd convinced her to join us. Turns out she was a lot of fun when she was off the job—though Joe still wasn't getting anywhere with her. She had brought out the hotel's portable stereo, and we were going to finally have the party on the beach that Nancy, George, and Bess had been hoping for all week.

"Wow," I said as I sat down in front of the stone-lined fire pit, a little bit away from everyone else.

"What?" asked Nancy, who had plopped down in the sand next to me.

"Nothing. Just . . . wow. I can't believe an ATAC agent would do something like this."

"What—do you guys believe anything just because it has ATAC's name on it? Isn't that kind of the opposite of what they teach you? To always be thinking for yourself?" She punched me lightly on the shoulder.

I blushed. Nancy had a point. And I wasn't good at being teased by girls. I changed the subject, fast.

"So what did Mr. Thorton say about Nikitin?" Nancy had been the one to explain everything to Mr. Thorton—leaving out the whole ATAC conspiracy part.

"Well, he wasn't involved in any of the violence, and it seems like Matthias took advantage of his desperation and concern about his family. But Mr. Thorton still felt like he couldn't keep him on as manager, so he's demoted him to desk clerk. Mr. Thorton thinks he got as much punishment as he deserved by nearly dying in the swamp."

"That was good of him." Mr. Thorton really seemed to care about his workers. "And Petrovitch?" I asked.

"After Mr. Thorton let his brother off, Petrovitch was incredibly thankful. Mr. Thorton promoted him to be the head of the Wetlands Spa. And he's paying for him to take some anger-management lessons!"

"Hey, guys, guess what?" George had put down the firewood and was frantically clicking away on her cell phone. We all stopped what we were doing and looked up at her.

"Turn on the news on the radio, Thatcher!" she yelled.

Thatcher fiddled with the dials for a second before pulling up a news station. There was a blast of static, and then a voice cut through.

"For all of you just joining us, the reports you've heard are true. Singing sensation Jasmina has come out of her coma and is reported to be in stable condition! We'll have more details as they become available."

We all cheered. Now it really was a perfect night at the beach.

Here is a sneak peek at the first exciting book
in the Nancy Drew Identity Mystery Trilogy:

Secret Identity

I s this the sort of romantic dinner you had in mind?" I couldn't help but smile as my boyfriend Ned took my hand and whispered to me as we moved into his dining room for dinner. We'd been apart for a week, since I'd been on a supercomplicated case that had brought me to New York, and had planned to make tonight our official "catch-up date" at our favorite Italian restaurant. But this afternoon Ned had called with a change in plans: there'd been a mix-up with faculty housing at the university, so he volunteered to host a visiting professor from Iran and his family at the Nickerson home. They wanted to have a small dinner to welcome them, and tonight was the only night that worked for everyone.

I leaned in close to him. "Romance, shromance. A piece of your mother's apple pie will make up for anything we missed."

Ned chuckled and squeezed my hand. "Maybe so. But we'll have to plan a make-up date."

"Agreed." I squeezed back and smiled.

The truth was, it still felt nice to be back in River Heights and doing all the normal things I like to do that don't involve cab chases or setting things on fire. My most recent case had turned into something bigger and crazier than I ever could have anticipated, and I was enjoying being "Normal Nancy" again, instead of "Action Hero Nancy." Being back in Ned's house felt wonderful. And the Nickersons' new houseguests, Professor Mirza al-Fulani and his daughter, Arij, who was twelve, plus his son, Ibrahim, who was sixteen, just couldn't be nicer.

"So, Nancy," Ibrahim began with a smile as we sat down at the dining room table, "have your travels for investigations ever taken you out of the country? Have you been to the Middle East at all?"

I smiled. The al-Fulanis were from Iran, and I was enjoying Ibrahim's upbeat attempts to understand American culture. "I'm afraid not, Ibrahim. I don't get the chance to travel all that much, even within the United States. But I would love to visit the Middle East someday. There's so much history there."

Professor al-Fulani smiled at me. "This is true, Nancy. It is still sometimes strange for my children and I to wrap our heads around American history, because your country is so new. So much has changed in only two hundred years, whereas in our part of the world, there are thousands of years of history."

Ibrahim piped up excitedly. "Will we study American history at the high school, Nancy?"

I nodded. "Actually, you will, Ibrahim. It's a required class for juniors."

"Excellent." Ibrahim dug into his salad with a grin, glancing at his sister. "I want to learn as much as I can about this country while we are here. I am so eager to meet my classmates."

Arij smiled and nodded, glancing at Ned and me. "Maybe you could look at the outfit I plan to wear tomorrow, Nancy," she said shyly. "I want to fit in well, and make friends quickly."

I laughed. "I don't know if I'm the best person to give fashion advice, but I'd be happy to offer my opinion!"

Ned squeezed my arm. "Don't sell yourself short, Nance," he cautioned. "After all, you are the reigning Miss Pretty Face River Heights!"

I rolled my eyes at him. While that was true, I wasn't exactly aching to talk about my short and ill-fated career as a pageant queen, which had been part of the case I'd been investigating in New York City. Still, he was smiling. I knew he found my totally out-of-character pageant win amusing.

"Nancy," Ibrahim said, "I am curious about how you solve cases. You have told us a little about your unusual hobby, and I must ask: Do you wear disguises? Do you ever have to lie to people to get the information you need?"

I squirmed in my seat. Ibrahim's face was warm and open, and I knew his questions were coming from an honest curiosity. Still, I liked to keep my trade secrets and didn't exactly want to confess to bending the truth in the service of, well, the truth in front of Ned's father and a bunch of people I'd just met.

"Let's just say I do what the case requires,"

I replied, reaching for the bread basket. "Every case is different. More bread, anybody?"

Mrs. Nickerson chuckled.

"Ibrahim and Arij," Ned cut in smoothly, "have you ever been to an American high school before, or will tomorrow be your first time?"

"Oh no," Ibrahim replied, shaking his head. "We have attended school in America before. My father travels often for work, you know, and we have traveled with him for months at a time."

Professor al-Fulani nodded. "My children lived with me while I taught at a university in Wisconsin, and also briefly in Florida. Unfortunately both placements were only for a few months, so they weren't able to settle in as much as they would have liked."

Arij nodded, pushing her salad around on her plate. "Sometimes it's hard to make friends," she admitted, a note of sadness creeping into her voice. "People hear my accent or they see my hijab and they think . . . They think I am something that I am not."

Silence bloomed around the table. I nodded sympathetically, imagining how difficult it must be for Arij and Ibrahim to fit in.

"I don't think that will be the case here, Arij,"

Ned said in a warm voice. "At least, I hope not. We're a university town, and used to diversity."

Mr. Nickerson cleared his throat. "You have any trouble, Arij or Ibrahim, and you let me know," he added. "Ned and I will do everything we can to make your stay here as pleasant as possible."

Arij smiled. She looked a little relieved. "I can't wait to meet everyone," she said quietly.

"Ibrahim and Arij seem very nice," I remarked to Ned a couple hours later as we stood on his porch to say our good nights. "I think they'll enjoy living here, don't you? I think they'll have a good experience at the high school."

Ned nodded. "I hope so," he admitted. "They're definitely a couple of great kids—so friendly and curious. I think as long as their classmates give them a chance, they'll have plenty of friends."

I nodded. The night was growing darker, and crickets chirped in the distance. I took a deep breath. River Heights, I thought happily. Home.

"So . . . ," Ned began, reaching out to squeeze my hand.

"So," I repeated, looking up at him with a smile. "Dinner? Later this week? Just the two of us?"

Ned grinned and nodded. "I'll call you," he said, leaning over to give me a peck on the cheek. "I'm so glad you're back, safe and sound."

"Me too," I said honestly, squeezing his hand again. "Thank your mom for dinner. It was delicious."

Stepping down onto the driveway, I pulled out the keys to my hybrid car and felt a wave of exhaustion wash over me. I imagined my nice warm bed at home, beckoning me. Without a case or anything urgent on the agenda, I could sleep in a bit tomorrow, too. I sighed, carefully driving through the streets that led me home. What a relief to be back among the people I loved, and with a little downtime.

At home, I parked the car in our driveway and yawned as I walked around to the back door. I felt like I had tunnel vision—all I could see was the route to my bedroom, where I'd soon be off to dreamland. Which is why I didn't notice that the kitchen light was on. And three people were sitting at the kitchen table, watching me curiously.

"Nancy?"

A familiar voice pulled me out of my tunnel vision, and I turned to find an unusual sight: my friend Bess; her twelve-year-old sister, Maggie; and our housekeeper and unofficial member of the family, Hannah, were munching on oatmeal-raisin cookies.

"Bess?" I asked, walking in. What on Earth?

Bess stood, placing her hand on Maggie's shoulder. "We were waiting for you to come home," she said. "Hope you're not too tired, Nance. Because I think we've got a case for you."

And here is a sneak peek at the first exciting book in the Hardy Boys Double Danger Trilogy:

Double Trouble

JOE

I could hear Bucky whinnying at me impatiently. "I'm coming, I'm coming," I muttered as I ran toward the horse. I untied him from the stump where my brother, Frank, had left him for me, then mounted up as fast as I could.

Bucky gave a little hop as I slid into the saddle. Horses don't get named Bucky for nothing. I urged him forward with my heels and we were off. Somewhere up ahead, Frank was running. We were in the middle of an all-teen Ride 'n Tie race.

Frank, Bucky, and I had already relayed our way more than twenty miles. Good thing ATAC agents have to stay in shape.

ATAC—that's American Teens Against Crime—had assigned us the mission of finding a saboteur. At the last Ride 'n Tie, the course had been sabotaged. A horse had ended up badly injured. And its rider had ended up dead. ATAC had reason to believe this racecourse would be sabotaged too.

So far, nothing.

I stayed on alert as Bucky trotted down the path through the woods. A Ride 'n Tie is all about endurance—for the horses and the humans. Anyone who gallops—or sprints—is going to end up losing. There were fifty more miles of trail to go. Horses and runners were spread out all along the course.

We rounded a corner—and Bucky reared. I almost slid off of him.

"Whoa! Easy!" I cried. But Bucky was freaked. He reared again, letting out a high, panicked whinny. I scanned the area, trying to figure out what was causing Bucky's agitation.

Rattlesnake! Right on the path in front of us. Its head was arched up in strike position, the rattle on its tail shaking out a warning.

I twisted around and managed to pull a can of energy drink out of the saddlebag. It wasn't that heavy, but I thought it might be heavy enough. I took aim and hurled the can at the snake.

The motion scared Bucky as much as the snake did. He hopped sideways to the right in a move I didn't even know a horse could make. Then he reared up again, so high I thought he would topple backward.

He didn't.

But I did.

I landed in the dirt with a thud. Snake! Where was the snake?

And then I spotted it—just a few feet away from me. Lying motionless. I'd killed it. I picked it up and hurled it off the path. "It's gone, Bucky, okay. It's gone." He stomped his front hooves. His eyes rolled, showing white at the edges. "It's gone," I said again. Then I reached out and managed to snag Bucky's reins.

I walked him in a circle, giving him time to calm down. "Ready to go on?" I asked. Bucky snorted. I took that as a not-quite-yet and walked him in another circle. That's when I noticed the sun spark off something metallic a few feet away, not far off the trail.

I tied Bucky to the nearest tree, then headed over to check it out. I found a metal cage, about the size to hold a rabbit. But there wasn't a bunny inside. There were three more rattlers. And the cage door—it was open.

I broke a small branch off one of the trees and used it to shut the door. Then I studied the area. Yeah, there it was. I knew there'd be evidence. On the trunk of the tree I'd broken the branch off was a smear of greasepaint. A mix of purple and pink.

At the start of the Ride 'n Tie, all the horses were tied at the far end of a meadow. A lot of racers marked up their horses with greasepaint or tied bright ribbons on them to make them easier to pick out at a distance.

Only one person had used pink and purple paint. I knew who the saboteur was.

I headed back toward Bucky, making a lot of noise so any other snakes that had escaped from the cage knew to get out of the way.

"The rules are changing a little bit, Bucky," I told him as I untied his reins from the tree. I climbed into the saddle. "Now we're going to go fast. Let's see what you can do." I tapped my heels into his sides a couple of times and we were off. Galloping down the trail.

I leaned forward, keeping close to Bucky's body.

"Frank!" I shouted when I spotted my brother up ahead. He stopped jogging and turned back. "We've got sabotage. And I know who did it." I brought

Bucky to a stop, and Frank leaped up on the saddle behind me.

"Okay, Bucky, mush!" I cried, giving the reins a shake. And Bucky mushed good. Dust flew up off the trail as he galloped.

I saw a horse and rider up ahead. Not the horse—or rider—I was looking for. I pulled the reins to the left and we galloped past.

"You're never going to make it to the end like that!" the rider shouted after us.

I didn't care about making it to the end. I just wanted to make it to the horse with the wild pink and purple flowers painted on its flank.

Bucky gave another whinny. And it wasn't the "hurry up" whinny. Or the "I'm scared out of my gourd" one. Nope, this was the happy, excited "I'm gonna see my girlfriend" sound.

"Get ready to rock and roll," I told Frank.

"I don't see anyone," he answered.

"You will," I said. I didn't need to urge Bucky to pick up speed. His girlfriend was up there, and that's where he wanted to be.

He sped around a curve in the trail. And, yep, there was Amber, Bucky's special lady with the pink and purple flowers on her hip. Ridden by Lisa, the saboteur. It didn't take us long to catch up to them. Amber was trotting and Bucky was galloping. At least until he reached her; then he slowed down to match her pace.

"Uh, hi," Lisa said. "You know it's cheating for both of you to be riding at once."

"Huh, I didn't think you'd be such a rule follower," I commented. "Since you left that cage full of rattle-snakes next to the trail."

Lisa didn't answer. Instead she dug her heels into Amber's side, and they took off at a gallop.

Bucky wasn't having that. He started galloping after them. He reached his girlfriend's side in seconds.

"Get as close as you can," Frank shouted.

Bucky was fine with close. My leg was almost bumping into Lisa's.

That's when Frank made his move. One second he was sitting behind me. Next he was behind Lisa, reaching around her to take the reins and signal Amber to stop.

Bucky stopped too. He gave Amber's muzzle a nuzzle. He was a happy boy. Frank and I were happy boys too. Mission accomplished.

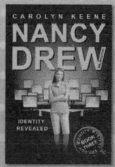
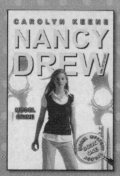
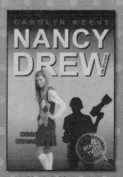